Craving
Passion
Sexy
Stories
Collection

VOLUME 23

10 EROTIC SHORT STORIES

ARIELLE FOSSETT

Craving Passion/ Arielle Fossett. -- 1st ed.
Xplicit Press, an imprint of TLM Media LLC

ISBN-13: 978-1-62327-554-9
ISBN-10: 1-62327-554-7
eISBN: 978-1-62327-604-1

Printed in the United States of America

CONTENTS

1 THREATS AND SEX

When Jerry met his wife she was a gorgeous brunette with luscious curls edging her small face. She had big blue eyes surrounded by the darkest ebony mascara, a tight ass and importantly, massive boobs. A woman every guy would love to fuck. She was happy to screw him on the kitchen bench, offer blowjobs in the backseat of the car...shit, she would even do anal.

After several years of hard work, raising children, and marriage, Jerry grew tired of his wife, who now appeared boring and unappealing, not like she used to be.

Finding he was visiting many porn websites and watching the videos for hours only one thing roamed his mind: "Fuck, I wish my wife did that."

While visiting a website, an ad popped up with a hot naked girl playing gently with her pussy. After watching for several seconds, a page came up asking for credit card details to see this girl put her fingers where every man wants to see them go.

Without hesitation and feeling so hard, he accepted and paid a fee.

He told his friends about this website and they suggested he go to a strip club instead and see it in person.

He told his wife he had a new job requiring him to work every Friday night, and she believed this until she read the credit card slips he was hiding under the mattress.

Realizing her relationship could be on the line, she knew she had to be a sexy hot woman craving the roughest sex; he'd be bound to play the game.

Putting on her leopard skin G-string and a silky see-through gown, she started to feel a little randy herself.

She lay on the bed with her old box of toys and waited for Jerry to come home.

He pushed open the door to find her laying with her legs crossed across the bed. She started running her hands down her legs, letting a little of the gown reveal her body as he followed her hand.

She started biting her lips as she motioned with one finger for him to sit next to her, and he followed.

Pulling him down beside her, she looked at her gown asking him if he would he like to see what's underneath. He nodded, still in shock, as she asked him if he would like to fuck what's underneath this gown.

He started growing hard and didn't know what she was doing, but he wasn't complaining. He was fucking horny.

She was sliding the silky gown in between her thighs with a gentle motion as she started undoing his fly, edging her hand downward and clutching his cock hard between her hands. His heart was racing. Licking her lips in a sexy way she started caressing his neck and his chest, teasing his nipples with the tip of her tongue. Her lips were warm and soft and he just wanted them around his dick. Sliding her lips downward and latching onto his shaft, she could feel his pre-cum; warm, a little salty, but very familiar.

He held the back of her ponytail and pushed her head down further, leaving nothing to be heard but her muffled moans as he kept stuffing his cock in her mouth.

He pulsed hard as she moaned louder, and asked in a dirty tone if she would like a cumshake in her mouth. She nodded as he pushed in further, deep throating her hard. Sighing with relief, he pulled out watching his cum drip down her chin, watching her lick her lips, chin and cheek, not leaving any cum behind.

"Who's the boring little housewife now?" she sneered at her husband. As he went to answer, she smiled as she pushed his hands in between her thighs telling him it was time for her pussy licking session.

He started rubbing his fingers in and out of her clit, each time going in further and faster, as she moaned like a motherfucker. She spread her legs like a hot knife through butter and continued spreading further until Jerry's face was facing her genitals. He could smell her savory scent as he pushed his tongue in further, tasting her sweet pink flower and gently pulling at her clit and lips with his teeth.

Moisture was filling her quickly and she was moaning louder and pulling at her tits. She was horny as fuck, and whispered, "My cunt is shivering, lick it more!" He roamed his tongue around her warm, hot, sweet pussy sticking a finger in her ass to create more sexual tension.

She was really screaming by this point, and he was staring at her face moaning with pleasure. He wondered why the sudden change in his wife - not that he was going to question this – as he liked the new horny bitch that he planned to fuck so hard she'd crave him more.

His tongue broadened in and out real slow to tease her and keep her lusty as he planned to fuck the shit out of her and screw her silly. Just before he went to pull out, she squirted her juices all in his face. She then ran her index finger over his face and slowly inserted it into her mouth.

Her vagina continued to cream as he used his hand on her ass cheeks to push himself in deeper. "Bitch you need to be taught a lesson" he whispered. Standing up she motioned with one finger for him to follow her, walking into the lounge room and then got down on all fours. She turned to him and said, "Then fuck me like I've been a naughty girl! Stick it in and pound me hard!"

Without needing lubrication - she already had the wettest pussy and the wildest sex drive - he bent down and slid his cock inside her deep, juicy pussy. He couldn't remember how long ago it had been since she agreed to doggy style. He caressed her boobs, pulling them back tight, grabbing her hair and riding her like bull. She nudged in pain as he pulled her hair tighter. Fuck this bitch, she deserved this.

Jerry spread her puffy lips outwards more as he pushed in harder, slapping her ass cheeks to punish her. This grew boring soon after, so she led him to the couch where she bent down, smooching up her juices from his raging cock that craved to bolt her further. She sucked some more then begged him to attach himself to her lips, to her puffy pussy. She lay on the floor, spreading her legs to show off her accessories perfectly. She ran her finger down her neck and chest, heading down further to her pussy, letting her husband see every detail.

She inserted one finger and played with herself for a few minutes, but gradually the feeling lessoned as she added another finger and pushed then in so deep his mouth started to water.

They French kissed for a while sharing each other's juices, leaving a salty taste behind.

Jerry milled his cock hard into her scandalous wet pussy, this time trading places to she was on to, so she could dominate.

Sliding her pussy just over his knob real slow, he felt extremely hot and sweaty seeing the enjoyment in her face. He sat up with her riding his slung like she meant it. He pushed up as she pushed in, grounding his cock hard inside her. Pressure was building up inside him and he was close to blowing his load. And iIntense orgasm was starting to fire inside her as she felt his load unravel inside her. She lifted off of Jerry and started to insert her anal beads as cum was running down her thighs. She pushed each ball slowly inside, watching as Jerry started to get erect again, so much lust burning inside him. He wanted to fuck her again, over and over like a horny fucked animal.

She bent over in front of him, baring her balloon knotted ass full of beads. She asked Jerry if he would like to pull them out one by one, slowly. He was in shock. What the fuck had happened to her? From a boring housewife to now a horny fuck machine.

After every one had been pulled out, she turned to Jerry stating that she was going to do the washing. Confused, Jerry followed, watching that tight slender ass move in front of him.

She sat on the washing machine, turned it on, and started up her vibrator. Smiling, she stated that's how she did the washing. Jerry watched speechless as she inserted her dildo in and out, letting out a rage moan that nearly made him cum.

She pushed it in harder, faster, running her lips over her teeth as she grinned at him. "Come and try me," she said. She motioned for him to take the vibrator. Moving in his hands he quickly inserted it, feeling it slide in ever so easy. Fuck, she was drenched. Never did Jerry think watching other women and visiting sex sites would lead her to this raging fuck engine on queue.

She pushed his hand, inserting the vibrator into her anal region. Jerry couldn't believe she was this hot. She pulled her hair back; it was all messy, dirty, but totally sexy. He took the dildo from her as he whispered that he could fulfill her dreams better than her vibrator could. Jerry bent her over the sink and fucked her hard until she moaned, groaned and was filled by cum. "Take that, bitch," he murmured as he pulled out. They kissed and caressed again, and Jerry felt that he needed her to suck his cock once more.

They moved the scene to the kitchen table, where Jerry sat on the chair and let her taste each of their juices mixed together. He wanted to come all over her face. He wanted to squirt all over her neck, and he wanted her to appreciate his personalized pearl necklace.

Her heart thumping, his cock pounding, he watched the cum run to the back of her neck, sliding into her hair. Yes, her hair; those brunette curls had bounce again. Jerry actually stopped to notice the almond brown twinge she still had in them. Starring into those deep blue eyes again, Jerry had missed them, but no time for the mushy stuff - he wanted to fuck her crazy one last time.

He ran his fingers down her back, feeling her shiver. She felt achy and tender, something she hadn't felt in so many years. She wondered why she let things change. She started ball sacking him and sucking his cock like there was no fucking tomorrow. She was unstoppable.

Jerry asked her to put her tight leather on again, which just completely blew him away.

She agreed, returning with no underwear on, just the leather pants all tight, outlining her slender body and showing her ass cheeks pushed in together. He wanted to suck them, place his dick in between them, and fuck away until he blew all over her.

She stripped again giving Jerry a lap dance before shoving her ass in his face. "Do you want me to lick it?" Jerry excitedly asked. "No way, I want you to fuck it hard and fast. Fuck me like I'm a dirty little bitch." Placing his cock in between her cheeks, he fucked away proudly.

She groaned extremely loud, making Jerry harder as he drilled her cheeks. She loved it. She turned her head, smiling at him from the doggy position, and he couldn't help himself. He pulled out and squirted all over her face. She giggled and pulled her body away. She touched her face finding it sticky, wet and salty. She suggested a shower. "I'll wait for you here," Jerry replied

She was persistent to save water and suggested they shower together. The water felt warm, soothing their worked up sweaty skin. "Here, let me wash your back for you," she whispered in his ear. The harsh sponge and soapsuds running down his back felt sensational. They switched places as Jerry started washing his wife's back. She turned to him, stating she had dropped the soap. She bent over so far Jerry could no longer control the urge and shoved his hard dick right in her ring hole. He pushed her forward, her head lowered and leaning against the glass shower wall. She could feel some water enter her as he pulled out then pushed back in. Moaning, whining, she asked to stop, but Jerry pulsed in deeper, flogging her ass while warm water ran down her back.

The water started to run cold. Jerry finished his load, rinsed off and left to pour himself a hot cup of coffee.

His wife offered to make him something to eat, but the coffee was sufficient enough. After all the work, his stomach didn't feel like eating.

Jerry soon fell asleep at the kitchen table, his wife smiling to herself. She was happy to have worn him out, as she had obviously satisfied him, but she wasn't finished yet.

She gently pulled his cock out of the damp towel and starting caressing it, focusing on the knob where she then laid her tongue to wander. Jerry awoke to the tightest erection and his wife's muffled sucks. Jerry started moving back and forth, holding her tightly downwards.

She stood up, placing one leg over his shoulder. Jerry placed two fingers only two inches inside her, when she started crying, "Oh yes, put them in deeper!" He tapped her pussy with his thumb, only teasing, to get her aroused more than before. Using her hand, she forced his fingers inside of her where Jerry felt the wetness of her juices all around his fingers. "God please go faster, oh yes, yes!" That's when he felt her squirt all over his hand. This bitch was ready to go again.

She felt sincere and she kissed Jerry with the most passionate kiss she had in years, letting her tongue explore Jerry's mouth. He kissed her back, feeling as empty as he ever had. He defiantly felt like the happiest man alive, no question about that.

"Don't end there, come on, make me cum," she said in such a stern voice. Then she stared at him with pleading eyes to screw her more.

Walking to the bedroom, Jerry grabbed her ass cheeks tight and slapped her hard, leaving a small red mark. She sneered, "You want it rough do you? Let me ride you on top and I'll show you rough." By now, poor Jerry felt worn out, but still found the energy to get bagging again.

She slipped on top, rubbing her bare cunt against his cock knob that was craving her juices all over it.

She could feel the foreskin rubbing inside her as she put her hands on his shoulders and rode him out of town. She moaned, groaned, sweated, and ached as he touched her tits swayed impulsively out of control above him, nipples erect. She was horny.

She sucked his ear, nibbled at his moist lips and rocked gently as she stayed seated upon him.

She fucked his dick as she sucked his nipples, leaving her saliva drooling across his chest.

He craved the backwards cowgirl. She turned around without pulling out. This was sexy; her ass in Jerry's face, as he watched it plead up and down, getting the hell fucked out of it.

She screwed him harder, and as he was about to let go, she stopped, pulled out and walked out of the room. "What the fuck!" Jerry yelled, as he followed her out, his dick so close to eruption. She bent over the staircase holding her butt cheeks open with both hands, slowly spreading her legs wider so Jerry could enter easily. His penis slipped in so easy. This girl was hot, wet and sticky, and so full of mixed juice he longed to eat.

He slapped her ass and pulled her hair as she moaned over the staircase. She was such a flexible woman, as she lifted her leg to lean over the rail so Jerry could penetrate her deeper, thrusting his cock in out, in out.

He grabbed his cock hard, pulled it out, and pushed her down into doggy position on the floor. He spread her lips with his fingers and inserted his tongue. Sweet but savory taste in each mouthful of varied juices seemed to taste better. She enveloped her arms around his head as he strapped himself in further.

Rubbing his tongue over her clitoris, she asked Jerry to stick just one finger in to tease her. Her moans filled the air it got too much for her yearning, begging him to stick more fingers in. She squirmed, but he continued with only one finger. "I'll suck you again if you put more in!" she cried. "That's what I like to hear," Jerry sneered. Inserting two fingers, her moans filled the air along with her voice screaming, "Finger fuck me faster, faster! Oh god...."

A small line of cum swirled down her leg. Jerry lowered his head, slowly licking up the trickle turning her on even more.

She tasted sweet like pineapple, but with a little hint of spice. "I love you," she whispered with her usually cheeky grin. Jerry stuck his fingers back in, pounding her cunt hard with his thick masculine fingers. She loved it. It was sex neither of them would forget.

Her fingernails dug into his back. She was close. "Make me cum Jerry!" she screamed. "Make me cum all over your fingers!"

She turned her moans into frenzied growls as she clawed at his back like a wild animal.

Jerry continued to eat her pussy as she squirted juice after juice into his mouth, filling it with delicious creamed cum. They both fell to each side of each other, trying to catch their breath, sweat filling their skins. Tired and exhausted, they settled in the kitchen where she sipped tea and watched Jerry starring at her boobs. She smiled and asked Jerry to flop his dick onto the table, as she wanted to play with it. Was this woman a sex god from heaven or what?

She took chocolate sauce from the refrigerator and microwaved it for thirty seconds, then slowly tipped the edge, letting the warm chocolate sauce drizzle down Jerry's cock, sliding ever so sticky over the end of his knob. She then bent down, and with just the tip of her finger, curled a small amount of sauce around and smoothed it across her tongue as sexy as hell. Following, she fondled his tongue with hers, letting him taste the gorgeous chocolate sauce. He was licking his lips when she stroked her way down to his cock, where she pursued to lick every last reaming taste of chocolate sauce off his hard erect penis. She sucked, curling her tongue around the base before heading on to flavor his balls with chocolate sauce now mixed with pre-cum.

Placing more chocolate sauce upon her tits, she asked Jerry to lick them clean as the sauce slowly dripped down her chest. She let it trickle down across her stomach, which he urged, craved, and yearned to lick. Legs spread, he could smell her scent. Smiling ever so sweetly, she fondled more with his wet sticky cock before asking him to fuck her on the bench. On her hands and knees she begged, "Fuck me Jerry, screw me like a bitch." He opened her legs, grinning at everything down there.

"That's a fine looking cunt," he said under his breath. He grabbed her hips tight and pushed her close to his body, penetrating her bottom. She started biting his shoulder, his lips, and then the nipples, tweaking and pulling them ever so gently. Gentle she was, but raging robust he was. Drilling his cock into her moist loveable pussy, she turned, telling him to ram it in her ass. She screamed that she wanted him to fuck her asshole; she wanted to feel him explode inside of her. He hammered her ass and buried himself inside of her, feeling her tight around him. He pulled out, cumming all over her back, rubbing his cum in and around her pussy and tapping her clit, pulling the lips apart revealing a perfect view of her pink erupting flower covered in sperm. The scent of her open pussy lingered; this woman was his personal fuck, a dirty whore who craved more.

Grabbing his cock hard once more, and pulling furiously with high friction, she pulled him rigid bringing a little painful feeling, but she was going off her tits, so he let her do what pleased her. Why ruin the moment?

Feeling exhausted, both of them collapsed back on their king sized bed, nearly falling asleep together. She leaned over and kissed Jerry on the cheek, turning her back to him and offering herself to be spooned. Jerry obliged, gently rocking her forward before finishing. Jerry pulled out, rolled onto his wife and passionately kissed her lips that now tasted delicious and still softly warm.

Staring her in the face, he noticed the true beauty he had forgotten all about. He ran his fingers through her luscious curls full of life as her eyes those bluest shades captured her lust.

A beautiful body. He wondered why he only had noticed now. Was their relationship back on track? Was this massive, sex-addicted girl going to continue to fuck him every day, anywhere he wanted?

Was it the thought of other girls rooting him that changed her? A little bit of envied jealousy? Or perhaps the thought of him having his cock in someone else actually turned her on; perhaps she found this hot.

Falling asleep together, their naked bodies wrapped together enveloping each other's arms.

After several hours, Jerry woke up his wife by gently fiddling with her breasts and gently chewing on her nipples like lollipops. Sensual sex is always good, but their sensual sex soon turned dirty. She couldn't help herself. Jerry tweaking her nipples made her hunger for his lust. Not just feeling in love and a little frisky, but feeling erotic and dirty; a feeling she couldn't shake off after she had squirted a few times. She let him slip in behind her again, pulsating intimately inside her as he stroked the back of her neck with his mouth, nibbling upon her chin as she started to lament. Jerry ran his fingers around her ass cheeks as she sighed with the feeling of being touched this way. He slowed his pulsing erection to tease her, lightly flowing inside then out, paying detailed attention to her clit, now lusty and swollen. Her thirst for him continued as she bent her arm over his side, pushing his hips closer to hers, bringing body heat and sweat closer. She could feel his hot breath on the back of her neck, making small hairs stand on end. She moved away, trailing her tongue downwards. Shit, she was going to the dive again. As she deep throated Jerry's six inches, she was so far down she was trying not to gag. She found his cum suddenly roaming her tonsils and dripping its way down her throat. Jerry watched his cum drool across her lips, and grabbed the bed sheet. He softly wiped his cum from her face, kissing her sweetly on the cheek.

"Best sex ever babe, don't ever change." She smiled and kissed him back, letting him embrace her on his naked lap. Falling asleep together, their naked bodies shared each other's sweat and left over juices. A few perfect sex scenes that very few men get to have. Not even his friends had told sex stories anything like this. His cock was numb, his lips were sore; muscles ached as her clit still swelled and her nipples were red and exhausted. Falling asleep in the midnight darkness, the sex had lasted all day and so many rooms were christened with their sex, including the kitchen bench and the washing machine.

Jerry had plans for the car next. He craved a blowjob while driving, craved sex in public, and craved bending his girl over the car hood. Plenty more ideas he planned to share with his wife.

A lonely husband who had a boring wife no longer needs to search the websites or continue his part-time job on a Friday night. He had back his MILF that everyone wanted after he'd finished telling his story.

2 BUSTY HOUSEWIVES RAGING SEX DRIVE

Susan had worked in the business as an administration clerk for several years. Just the other day, Susan's boss called her into his office and explained that there was another clerk coming on board to join their team. Susan was fine with this. That was until she met him. Dan arrived on time with his briefcase and black pointed toe shoes. He had a shaved number two haircut with blonde tips; she guessed he was in his early thirties, about the same age as her. His face had no imperfections visible and she noticed his smile straightaway. It was certainly one to remember.

Now Susan had a dirty mind, and

watching his hand shake hers, she noticed his long, smooth fingers. She was not thinking along the lines of what nice hands he has or comments like "wow his hands are so smooth." The opinion she had in mind was, "fuck, imagine those fingers inside me." Susan loved sex; she loved everything about it. She had a happy marriage, but her husband Joe's sex life was not as exciting as it used to be. He used to turn her on but not much anymore. Susan changed her way to suit her sex life; Susan was not a cheater. She hadn't ever slept with anyone while married to her husband, but she had made some changes.

Susan now needed stimulation; she needed something to make her feel horny before she had sex with her husband. Pornos were her best friends along with her close buddy, her vibrating dildo.

Susan felt she needed these to enhance her sex life. Susan could have anyone she wanted, and she could make them keep secrets for her if she only asked. Her beautiful brunette curls hung just under her shoulders. Red lipstick suckered her pouty lips. Sexy smooth legs led down to elegant feet in heels. She was pure beauty. Sure enough she had men who tried flirting with her; she had men that wanted to take her out for friendly drinks but never did she satisfy herself and said yes.

This new assistant had noticed her beauty; he smiled at her as she saw his eyes dwindle down to her chest. No wonder! She was a very busty woman, with breasts anyone would yearn for.

After several days turning up to work feeling drained—and sexually frustrated—Susan was very moody.

She arrived a little bit earlier than usual to catch up on a few invoices that were overdue and needed to be sent out. She was tenderized when she noticed Dan starring at her. He had gorgeous eyes she only came to notice when he bent over her, reaching for his paperwork. She knew it was a deliberate act. He could have easily gone around the opposite side, but perhaps he wanted to catch a glimpse of her eyes or smell her scent. Susan felt very flushed and warm each time Dan brushed up against her. It was also the fact that she hadn't had intimate sex with her husband for several months; she just couldn't get horned up enough.

Dan proposed a drink at the local cottage bar—just the two of them. He explained that he wasn't from this part of the country and could do with a guide around the local attractions. Seeing as he was going to be her partner at the office, it was probably better to break the ice now and get to know him somewhere more social rather than at work.

Susan headed home and explained to her husband what the plans were; they had a trusting relationship and her husband, Joe, didn't have any bother with this. Dan had offered to pick Susan up, as he was a gentleman. He arrived at her house around 7PM. He was well dressed, wearing a tight blue shirt that carved in his chest muscles. Susan had a red necktie tee that matched her glossy lips and black leather pants that framed her tight ass perfectly. When she walked, her ass outline was perfectly able to be seen. She had long nails, with polish shaded to match her tee. A perfect woman who left every guy craving for her.

She let Dan lead the way into the bar where she ordered whisky on the rocks.

She watched Dan closely as he seemed to study her, looking her up and down not in an awkward way but in a more impressive way.

Soon enough, they talked about relationships and lovers. Susan had explained that she was happily married for years. Dan commented like he knew all about her life, "Some people are happily married but their sex life sucks." Susan was surprised; she looked away smiling.

She couldn't have agreed more. Dan was divorced. He left his wife after their sex life turned to the point where they didn't even have one. He obviously didn't want to try to find a way to make it exciting; he just decided to leave it.

Susan didn't want to talk more on that subject so she decided to check the menu for something to eat. Dan excused himself from the table and headed towards the men's room.

Then she felt a brush against her shoulder; Dan had returned and was resting his hand quite sensually on her shoulder. She brushed him off and suggested they ordered dinner.

Susan was talking about children; neither of them had any kids. Susan had preferred the quiet life as Dan had agreed.

Dan was quite intrigued about the way Susan's lips quietly begged to be kissed.

She watched his eyes as they made their way back to hers. Their gaze was interrupted when their meal was placed in front of them. Their meal was very enjoyable, as was, Dan would say, his view of Susan. He was starting to like her, as she felt about him. The night had gone quite quick after they had several conversations about work and their likes and dislikes.

Dan had soon dropped her home. They hadn't said too much on the drive home.

Dan waited in the car, making sure she had gone inside all right; she knew he was a bit of a sweetheart. She made herself and her husband a cup of tea before showering and heading to bed. Joe soon followed and crept into bed beside Susan. Leaning over, she kissed Joe goodnight. While she did this, all she could think of was Dan, even after she lay with her eyes closed.

The next morning Susan got coffee on the go and headed to work; the car didn't start straight away and she was late. Frustrated again! Dan could tell she was moody and thought he'd crack a joke, "Need a little bit of rough sex, do we?" Susan didn't find this funny, as it really was the problem. She needed hot sex from her husband.

Susan decided to eat her lunch outside away from everyone; she hated being moody and taking it out on other people.

She was enjoying the sun when Dan came up and sat down as if he was invited. He placed his hand on hers, asking if she was sexually frustrated.

"Why is that any of your business?" Susan asked angrily.

Dan looked straight at her without blinking. "I can help you out if you need me to. Our little secret."

Susan walked off in a huff. Great! Another coworker who wants to get into her bed. She didn't want work to be awkward, but it pretty much already had become that way. She spent last night thinking about Dan, and now she was thinking about what he said to her today. It kind of turned her on a little bit but she fully denied it of course.

Back in the office in front of the computer, an e-mail popped up on her screen:

"You want to take me up on my offer."

It didn't say whom it was from, but she knew it was from Dan. He didn't look at her while she read it, but she knew. She replied, "I'm happily married. Thank you."

The next reply was, "Well, in this case, sometimes you need a little more and perhaps I'm offering to help you out. Will be our little secret." Susan didn't reply. Her boss came out, stating they weren't able to finish work earlier due to technical failures in the system they used.

As Susan headed to her car, Dan followed her. "Would you like me to show you my new place?" Susan didn't want to go but it would probably shut him up if she did.

His house was beautiful, big, and impressive; she wondered if the sword in his pants was the same. She walked into his lounge and sat on the sofa. Dan took off his shirt and singlet as he was going for a swim. Susan watched him flex his muscles before jumping into the pool; he was certainly hot with no shirt on. Susan's fingers wanted to wander down below and her pussy felt like it was starting to swell.

She was horny and felt like playing with herself.

Dan got out of the pool, small beads of water sitting on the surface of his much-tanned skin. He gave her a smile as he walked by her—the type of smile that any woman would bend over for. Susan adjusted her large tits in her bra as she watched Dan stare deeply at her chest. Susan had called it a night soon after and asked her husband to pick her up from Dan's house, to which he agreed. It was a little awkward as Susan said goodbye to Dan. She got the feeling he wanted to rip her clothes off and drag her to bed. She talked with her husband about the experience, stating that he was a nice man and that they should all meet up for a drink sometime.

The next day at work, Susan seemed to be in a bit better mood but still easily frustrated. Dan bought her an instant coffee from the machine outside the hall. As he leaned across Susan to place her coffee on the desk, he started to smell her scent. "You smell like a goddess," he whispered close to her cheek. He knew ways to get to a girl's heart, as he knew how to turn a woman on. She trusted he knew he was hard to resist. She watched him during the day running over scenarios in her head—how she'd love to get her hands on his towering love pistol and even how she'd love to taste his swollen zesty love trumpet. Susan had quite a dirty mind, especially when it came to a hot man's crotch accessories.

She watched in detail as Dan bent over the copy machine, revealing the outline of his perky ass cheeks. She slid past him trying to get a better view as she sipped her coffee. He knew she was watching; he knew she wondered about his bedroom skills.

They were comparing notes of the latest assessment. Dan was sitting quite closely to Susan and was breathing warm air on the back of her neck. Seeing her deep in concentration, he ran his fingers over hers, sending shivers through her body. She felt herself becoming hot, aroused, up to wanting her partner's male counterparts. Pulling at her collared shirt, she was feeling moist in several parts of her body. Knowing it was soon lunch break, she asked the boss if she could leave earlier.

He didn't mind but Dan seemed to; he asked her where she was going and why. Susan had something in mind: she was going home to play with her husband's engorged cock. Dan had helped her reach her arousal, making her pussy swollen and her wanting now to fuck her husband.

Walking in through the door, she didn't hesitate to take her shoes and jacket off.

Her hubby was watching TV as he had a week off work. She walked over in front of the TV and started stripping her clothes off. She had his full attention. Susan was stripping with a nice little pose. Gnawing her lips and massaging her breasts, she strutted over to him and sat right on his lap. She could feel his cock rising hard as she rubbed herself on his lap. He pulsated, throbbed, and ached; she was looking sexy and he wanted a piece of her.

Her phone vibrated, and she leaned over to read it. It was a message from Dan. He must have got her number from her file.

"I'm thinking we should hook up. You know you want to."

After reading that, Susan was extremely turned on that she wanted to feel the heavy pressure of his drill in her hands—and inside her wet mutt. She wanted him to insert into her moist bounty where her cream could be unleashed.

Dan replied through text afterwards: "I want to be inside you and feel your cum all over my cock."

Reading this message twice, she felt her cunt become wet and swollen and felt like sucking her hubby's cock as if there was nothing to lose. Susan slid herself off his lap and sat couched on the floor at his feet. She fondled his hard cock in one hand as she pulled his pants to his knees with the other. She teased his sword in her hands and ran the tip of her finger right down to the end of his shaft, then moving her mouth closer to take it in whole.

Her husband said she was good at deep throating: she could put the whole cock in her mouth and not gag. She pushed it in deeper so she could let the precum drip down her tongue. She drove it in harder and faster, sliding her tongue down and up as she sucked away.

She could feel him throb inside her mouth, with loads of warm moist precum dripping on her lips as he was very close to blowing his load everywhere around her mouth. She pushed him in further and sucked the tip of his knob roughly as he cummed all over her face. Liquid, zesty, salty moistness was everywhere. She licked her lips, tasting his glory. She wanted more.

It was time for him to plunge deep into her honey center; she wanted him to make her honey pot melt with his fingers, his cock, and his tongue. She wanted it all.

She stripped off her pants, letting them fall to her feet. She bent over in front of her hubby and told him to play with her tight humid box. He pinched her pussy lips and pulled at them with his teeth; she had long pink-coloured lips her hubby adored.

She kept sending dirty messages to Dan as her husband had buried his head deep inside her pussy.

He admitted he wanted to fuck her brains out; he wanted to lick her purring kitty and find her deep pleasure spots.

She thought about Dan as her hubby ate her out, creating cream after cream of cum. Her nectar was soaking her pussy and her thighs. Susan moaned like she hadn't before; she let herself go just wild. She felt dirty and filthy.

Her music box was getting a ride with his tongue as her phone was constantly vibrating with messages from Dan. "Please let me fuck you from behind, you filthy whore."

With that comment, Susan got on all fours and begged her husband to fuck her from behind.

As he inserted his steel manhood into her small enveloping pussy, her cunt swelled around his hard, erect, engorged schlong. It tightened and swelled as she pushed herself back against him, allowing his cock to penetrate her wet fanny deeper. She craved his cock; her pussy bites for his dick.

He climbed on top of her and pounded her as if she were a wondrous whore who needs to be taught a lesson. Susan moaned and groaned, grabbing at his back, pushing him in further, drowning his cock inside her drenched pussy.

His tower pushed exclusively inside of her, her thinking of Dan as she cummed three times in a row. Once he got Susan going, she went hardcore. She didn't like foreplay; she went straight to dick and pussy action. As he climbed off her, he glided his tongue down her body and over her breasts. He suckled her nipples, kissed her cheeks and tongue-actioned her mouth. She was hot and horny and was thinking about Dan.

Susan whispered begging in his ear to take her ass from behind and plunge it hard. Susan bent over and backed her ass up towards him. He placed his hard cock in between her ass cheeks and started rubbing in between. He went faster and harder as he slid a finger in Susan's pussy from behind. He fucked her cunt roughly with his middle finger; she groaned loudly when he cummed all over her slender ass cheeks. His juice dripped, dribbled, and slipped down her crack, running into her pussy, then down her thigh. His fingers devoured her kitty and her cum ran freely.

She was drenched, soaked and begging for an ass flogging. He fingered her tight little knot until her juice lubricated the spot. He then inserted his flogged-up hot Joe into her damp hole and fucked her away, slapping her ass firmly as his cock pulsated inside her tight passage. His rock-hard bulging shaft increased in size as he made that tight hole become loose. She was a delicate feather that he tore apart. Her tits bounced to the rhythm of his fuckable motion. Pulling her ass closer to him, his cock pushed in, piercing her further; there was no dildo that could compare to this pistol she now had full control of. His steel hammer exploded its cream inside her; she moved her ass backwards and let the cream run from her knotted hole.

This wasn't enough. Susan led her husband to the lounge suite where she planned on having more fun. This was the place Dan had told Susan he was going to fuck her silly. Susan wanted her husband to plunge his tongue deep inside her pussy while she bent over the couch. Her happy box was puffy, her lips enlarging. She was nearly numb but pleaded to be licked out until she was.

She bent over very far; she was a very flexible girl. She fingered herself, teasing her hubby as she licked her fingers clean. He didn't want the teasing. He couldn't handle the teasing. He took her hips in his rough hands and pushed her body towards him as he screwed his tongue far into her moist pussy. She automatically impaled her cum in his face; he curled his tongue and tapped her pussyhood with his tongue. She squealed with excitement. She wanted his fingers, his cock—anything— inside her again.

She grabbed his pole and pushed it inside her. She forced his cock to stay in her and drill her forcefully. She was so horny that she wanted to be fucked again, red, raw and numb, but she'd still take it any way it came.

The next day Susan was sore and tired and her muscles ached. Heading to work, Dan greeted her at the door with a cup of coffee. She took it from him without looking at him. She felt a little awkward. She'd got hot and horny and fucked her husband time after time as she was thinking about Dan. She didn't want to have sex with him, but fuck he turned her on and that was enough for wild sex with her husband.

Dan swept by her and placed a hand on her shoulder. "I loved those messages last night." Susan smiled; what could she possibly say back to that?

She knew that when she walked in front of him, his eyes were glued to that petite little ass of hers that he so desperately wanted to get his hands on.

Dan was sending her more dirty

messages throughout the day, and she was severely aroused. She was easily led to becoming wet when her mind was on Dan. Susan watched Dan sip his coffee when she noticed him licking the edge of the cup; she also noticed the tongue action she'd love to get a bit of on her pussy. He rounded it, curled it, and moistened it. Imagine what he could do with it inside her mutt. The scenarios of these situations flowed through her head as she sat there, undressing him in her head and thinking how she'd fuck the shit out of him.

She could feel her nipples becoming erect as these images ran through her head. Perhaps these thoughts were okay as she wasn't actually fucking Dan—just having very lustful thoughts of Dan. She ordered him to get her more coffee just so she could see that ass walk past her. He returned with no coffee; Susan questioned this. Dan's answer was a kiss on the back of her neck.

Suddenly Susan felt warm as she was having hot flushes. She turned away. She couldn't do this. She had never been unfaithful to her husband. Dan moved closer, pinning her to the wall so that she couldn't move away from him. He kissed her cheek and her lips as he led her hand to feel his hard erection. Susan could no longer hold from the temptation after she felt his raging cock. He was hard and huge. She kissed him as she ripped his shirt off. The thoughts of her husband had disappeared for a short time while she was in the arms of Dan. Susan pushed everything off her desk, slid onto the top and spread her legs. She motioned for Dan to go down on her. He obeyed. Susan had him so horned up he felt he couldn't say no, his cock yearning her pussy, her hands, her touch.

The passion and lust was soaring and Susan had never felt another cock as big as this one. While Dan did what he did inside her crazy, horny pussy, Susan texted her husband a very sexy message that was very intimate and very detailed. Dan worked his magic with his tongue inside her wet fur burger.

She moaned and pushed his head to go deeper. He knew the spot to hit.

She helped Dan's erection pulse harder as she grabbed him in her tight hands and jerked him hard. Pulling with force, her hands grew tighter around him as he swelled more. Dan was close to blowing when she stopped, got down lower and gave him the best blowjob he'd ever had, focusing on the knob where she sucked so hard he felt the pressure. His cum had blown all over everywhere.

Susan went home sticky and moist, greeting her husband at the front door where he waited for her surprise at the text message she had sent him. He read it back to her. She had been too horny to realize what she had written. He didn't question this; he was turned on by it. Susan took her husband and ripped his shirt off, and tongued him for over two minutes.

She had extreme fun having sexual encounters with Dan, but her husband's cock was hers as her wet horny pussy shall only be his. Well, this is what she told her husband. Those encounters did occur quite recently with Dan and also with the three other assistants who were hired after Dan had been fired due to being caught using his phone during work hours.

Each assistant was fired and the boss decided not to rehire so that was Susan's chance to become faithful to her husband again. The arousing text messages with Dan and the other boys did continue, but that's all that they continued to be. Susan just often needed a little lust in her life—a little bit of harmful secrets to make her a qualified fucking agent that was extremely hot with the best fucking tits any man would pay to have.

3 STRAIT TO SWINGING ORGIES

I am fully supportive of my husband, but I wasn't feeling it when he came home this morning from his night shift job, telling me we were going to a friend's pool party. I am not into parties, especially pool parties.

I have been told I look good in a swimsuit. I guess it couldn't hurt, but I wanted to make sure I was up to scratch if I was going to be in a bikini.

I called up my friend and we headed out for a girl's day, pampering ourselves trying to get me in the mood for the party. First, we got our nails done, French tips, then we had lunch, laughing and joking about the hot fellas I would see at the party, especially the ones only wearing speedos on their bottom half.

I got my hair dyed and curled; I wasn't planning on getting it wet. I went black, and I think it looks good on black chicks; it brings out their eyes, especially if they have almond-shaped blue eyes, which is what I have. I had my eyebrows waxed and shaped and bought a new bikini.

I usually like ones that cover most of my body, but my friend Jess suggested this real sexy bikini. It only covered half my ass cheeks and the bust was low cut and revealing. After I had stared at it for a long time in the changing room, I pulled the curtain back half way asking Jess her opinion. Jess smiled, but before she could answer, this older man that looked about ten years older than me, around about forty, gave me a thumbs up saying it was hot.

I blushed at him; he smiled and said, "You have it, so flaunt it."

That did it. I was going to the party with this underneath.

I picked out a new pair of jeans that were really tight and a tank top that was covered in silver sequins. Perfect! I'll wear my bikini underneath and strip when I'm ready to swim.

After we had a coffee, Jess drove me home since I needed to sleep before I started on the scotch and rocks.

My husband woke me up at 7 p.m. I had slept since three o'clock. I rolled back over, but after he put a scotch under my nose, I was soon awake.

I showed him my new bikini after I had showered. I was standing naked. He was already getting an erection. He licked his lips and asked if he could pound my tight pussy with his 9-inch black cock.

Wow! This bikini was a god sent. He bent me over the sink, inserted his first two fingers and strapped my pussy hard until I became wet. He slid his cock quickly between my thighs, soon finding my opening and slithering himself inside.

He caressed my bare tits that were smothered in cocoa butter cream. I was hot and horny as he pushed his mouth around my nipples clutching tight with his lips and slowly pulling letting my nipple slid out of his grip. His skin was light brown, while mine was darker, and the two colors twisted together looked so sensual. His erect penis was pushing hard against me and I begged him to put it in my damp pussy.

He wanted to tease me a little longer, fiddling with my lips with the tips of his fingers and gnawed at my nipples. He pulled me closer rubbing his cock hard against me as I kissed him passionately. His black cock was throbbing and it was eager to be inside me.

He untied my bikini bra and let it drop to the floor as he slowly pulled my bottoms down. I stepped out of them. He kept nudging his cock up against me. I was at the point where I didn't want foreplay - I wanted to fuck, I wanted him to do me doggy style.

I could feel my cum dripping down my leg as I bent over in front of him.

"Fuck me, fuck me now!" I cried.

He ran his fingers in and out of my pussy and then began running his finger across my ass hole. As I became really wet, he stuck his black cock in hard and started thrusting back and forth. As he blew inside me, I glanced at his watch. We were going to be late if we didn't leave in the next fifteen minutes.

I quickly added some bronzer to my face. I didn't need much just that little touch, downed a few scotches and then we left. I was feeling a little tipsy when we arrived, and I was amazed at the amount of people that were there.

I noticed that my husband was already checking out the girls hanging out of their clothes, and might I add some had nice tits too.

We were greeted by Jenny and Stan. They were a lovely couple. We had met them on our trip to Hawaii, and finding out we lived only a few blocks away from each other, we became good friends.

We talked for a few minutes, and then they motioned for us to come in and meet a few of their friends. We got introduced to a stunning black couple, Juliana and John. They were both very attractive. My husband and Juliana were already off to a good start. I didn't mind when my husband flirted because I just started flirting as well. We weren't swingers, but sometimes it's good to flirt with strangers. I think it enhances our sex life.

Juliana's husband noticed that they were chatting each other up. He stood next to me commenting on my beautiful sequin top. Feeling a little naughty, I smiled and said, "You should check out what's underneath!" He laughed, "Well, do you care to show me"?

"Ha, later". I said, not knowing what later had in store for me.

All four of us headed over to get some cocktails and to get a towel for the pool. I was walking in front of Juliana and she wolf whistled at me commenting on my fine-looking ass; I shook it fast just to tease her a little.

She actually came up behind me and slapped my ass pretty forceful. I laughed, but I was still shocked. Not many women just go up and randomly slap another chick on the ass.

I wasn't offended just thought it was

different.

I skulled a few cocktails and headed over to the pool with Juliana and John. My husband had wandered off somewhere else. Juliana was taking her clothes off revealing a gorgeous body, but as I was stripping, and I noticed John staring at me.

Juliana headed over to the pool. I watched her perfect body; it was toned, all in line with no flaws. She dove in and I turned around to see John standing uncomfortably close to me. I stepped back from him. He smiled asking if he had upset me. I just said no. He apologized saying he couldn't help but to look closely at me, as I was a beautiful woman.

Being polite and getting myself out of that awkward situation, I headed over to the pool end that Juliana was relaxing in. I slowly wedged myself in the pool, being careful not to wet my hair. Juliana's skin looked amazing underwater. It glistened. My husband headed back over to us positioning himself next to Juliana as I was in between Juliana and John. I watched my husband stare at Juliana. I think he was interested in her. Did he forget he is married and his wife was right there? Maybe not. They got into another deep conversation as I felt what I thought was a hand rubbing my leg. Must just be the water. As I stared down, I realized it was a dark skinned hand belonging to John.

I didn't really know what to do. His wife was right next to me. I thought if I was to tell his wife he'd deny it, and I'd end up looking like a dick. His hand did feel good rubbing my skin underwater so I let him go. It really wasn't any harm.

I started to get turned on as John started rubbing my clit. It was wrong, awkward, but fuck it felt good. Juliana turned to me asking my opinion on their conversation I didn't know where to look; she's talking to me while her husband was playing with my clit. I looked at my husband. He didn't notice, and I really didn't want John to stop. I jerked forward a little when I felt John's finger slid inside my pussy letting in the cool water. Fuck! It felt perfect. His motion was very slow as to not make it obvious. He was talking to his wife like normal, as if nothing was going on right next to her.

Juliana asked if I wanted another cocktail.

"Please, I could do with one."

My husband told me he'd be back soon, he'd help Juliana with the drinks. I watched them walk away, and there was a quite noticeable chemistry between them. I think John noticed too. He inserted two fingers inside me. I was hoping no one could see, as wrong as it was it felt good and he was one hot black babe.

He leaned in closer and I could feel his erection on my side. I eased back; he whispered in my ear, "They are doing it we should, too."

I didn't believe him. My husband wouldn't. He took my hand, led me out of the pool and took me upstairs where I could hear people in different rooms having sex. He opened a few doors until he pointed saying, "Told you."

My husband was banging her black ass, and she was riding him hard. I turned to John asking if there was a spare room.

"So you wanna do it?" he asked.

"Of course, I want to do it; I'm going to fuck you better than she does."

He wrapped his arms round me, and we started making out, full of passion and sharing our tongues. We slipped in the hallway cupboard filled with jackets and coats. He flapped his cock hard against my leg. I asked him if he want a blowjob.

I got down on my knees as he hit my cheek with his hard cock. Opening my mouth, I asked him to insert his huge black dick into my mouth so I could make it cum. I teased a little running my tongue over the tip as I began sucking only the knob, sucking as I ran my tongue over his hole.

John grabbed the back of my hair gripping it tight he pushed my head forward, making his cock go in deep. I swayed back and forth dragging my tongue up and down his throbbing cock making him groan with pleasure. I sucked his balls as I started to feel him precum.

"Baby I can catch, and swallow".

He smiled pushing my head in far and fast. I could feel he was pulsing. He was close. I pulled my head back and opened my mouth where I felt his cum dripping down my chin. I swallowed like a good girl does and wiped my chin. John helped me up, but only half way; he then curved me over and shoved his huge black cock inside me. I was moaning loud inside that hallway closet. Fuck! He was good. He pulled nearly all the way out leaving just the knob inside me where he rocked a little sending out a little more cum.

John whispered in my ear, "Brace for impact."

I held on to the rack in front of me as he fucked me. Not much room in the broom closet, but we managed to screw each other in there. He finished blowing his load inside me. We stepped out of the closet and headed back to the party.

About ten minutes later, my husband and Juliana finally turned up saying there was a line at the drink stand. I just smiled. Juliana and her husband disappeared together. My husband asked if I had a good talk with John while he was gone. I laughed.

"Sure, did you have fun rooting Juliana's cunt?"

He starred at me with a blank expression. I then explained causally my encounter with John in the broom closet, coat cupboard whatever you want to call it.

He continued to just stare as I said, "Sharing is caring. You got a fuck, so did I. We're even".

We went to look for the hot couple. We searched a few rooms in the mansion house and found them doggy style, buck naked and fucking on the bed. I had obviously had too much alcohol because I pushed open the door and walked up to Juliana, forcing her to kiss me, saying it wasn't fair to fuck without me. I untied my bikini top and threw it at my husband who was silent at the doorway. I held my right tit in my hand leaning forward to John asking if he wanted to lick it. He fondled with my tits with his tongue while he fucked Juliana hard.

I pulled her hair saying, "Take it like a bitch! Let him fuck your brains out you whore."

My hubby walked over and stood in front of Juliana, who was still on all fours getting fucked from behind. I pulled his shorts down, telling Juliana to suck his cock and make him cum. She did as I asked.

John finished his load inside of her, and while we were waiting for the blowjob to finish, John and I dry fucked for a little bit, letting him feel my clit lips along his balls. I was horny, rough, and I wanted to fuck.

I moved my ass in the air and pushed my pussy onto to John and started to ride him like I was a dirty little whore.

He pulled my rack hard as I bent down so he could suck my nipples and gnaw at them. I was moaning loud and talking dirty in his ear and in no time he had cum everywhere inside me. I rolled off him and told Juliana to stop sucking my husband and come and eat her baby's cum out of me.

She didn't hesitate; she opened my legs and started eating his nectar. The men were so hard; both were throbbing red. I loved it. After I felt myself cum, I pulled her head up to mine where we shared a French kiss.

John grabbed her and pushed her downward telling her to get on all fours, as did my husband. John inserted his cock into my ass as my hunny stuck his in Juliana's.

"I'll race you," my hubby said to John.

They started fucking each others' girl from behind, and slapping our asses till they became red. They were too busy drilling us to notice Juliana and I signaling to each other. As they screamed they were about to cum, me and Julie pulled out and started to kiss. We then started jerking off the boys while on our knees, catching their cum in our mouths, then playing tonsil hockey with each other, sharing both juices together.

Juliana and I both agreed to head to the pool for a bit to relax and just talk. Sitting in the pool with her, I noticed her beauty. She was a hot little mama. I couldn't help myself; I started running my hands across her rack, and with the pool very crowded, no one noticed me going under the water and sucking her nipples.

We played with each other for about twenty minutes, until the men joined us in the pool again. Juliana and I dove down in the water and started playing with their cocks. They were hard and erect. We surfaced to see Jenny and Stan talking to the fellas, not noticing what we had been doing, thank god.

They asked us to get out of the pool; they were going to do a swimming race. "Awkward," I said out loud. The men had hard cocks getting out of the pool. Everyone would see. What had to be done had to be done. They got out of the pool hoping their shorts would shield them a little bit.

Embarrassed, we decided to leave the party and head home. We had to get a taxi. Each had drunk way too much. The taxi ride home was interesting. I had both men in the back with me. One was fingering my pussy, the other was getting a blowjob from me. Juliana distracted the driver revealing her huge tits for him to look at.

We were a bunch of horny fucks really, and we all had the same idea of going back to my house and firing up the erections again.

Our place was closer than Juliana's, so the less driving time, the quicker we get to fucking time.

Once the taxi had left, I fiddled in my bag drunk as a skunk to try and find my key, when I noticed Juliana was already making out with the two guys.

I got inside leaving them to finish outside. John walked behind me grabbing my sides and pushing him close to me. He was such a cutie.

I took his hand gently and led him upstairs to the drawer where I keep my toys. As we were making out spread on the bed, Juliana and my hubby walked in watching us. I motioned for Juliana to sit next to me. After she sat down, I pretended to rub her neck and her back, and I positioned her right to handcuff her to the bedposts.

I had her locked in position. She was quite shocked by this, especially as I told the two men to fuck her, one in the ass, one in the pussy while I sat on her face and let her lick me out. I loved the way she tasted me, the way she motioned her tongue around inside of me; she knew the spots to hit.

Handcuffed with both hands, being fucked in both holes and having a hot, drenched pussy on her face, she was in heaven. I told her to keep licking as I was close to cumming; John kindly asked me to squirt over Juliana's face, and I moaned as I was real close. She twisted her tongue, curled it, and penetrated deep; I lifted myself off her and let myself go. I had squirted pretty far also as the guys had blown their load in her.

She was a cum bucket and she loved it. John, panting, leaned over, grabbed my dildo and shoved it in my mouth. I deep throated the vibrator as he pushed anal beads in my ass. My moans were muffled from the dildo, I started to choke as he shoved it in so far. Ripping it out of my mouth, he shoved my face into Juliana's cunt and I started to taste her juice and smell her scent. Her legs were spread wide and I noticed her pussy was swollen. She was craving the cock. Slapping her pussy hood with my dildo, she begged me to put it in her. I pushed it in roughly and fucked her cute pussy until she cummed all over it. The sheets were drenched and we were all out of breath.

I opted out for a shower as the others just laid there. Letting the water drop down my back running past my legs, the room filled with steam pretty quick and I hadn't noticed John standing there watching me, until I wiped the steam from the glass wall of the shower. I opened the door, and he stepped in noticing the water was really hot. He made me turn around as he ran his hands through my long hair. I had now lost the curls.

He grabbed the conditioner and pulled it through my hair massaging my scalp. It felt good. I let the water run down my hair rinsing the conditioner off. My body became really glassy, slippery and soft from the conditioner. John started rubbing my hands over my tits. I turned around and kissed him. I placed my left leg up on his side and made his hard cock enter me. He lifted me a little to the right position and slowly swung in and out of my pussy. He finished as we watched the cum run down my leg into the water, pooling at the bottom of the shower. I licked John clean; I didn't want the rest from his penis going to waste. He was loving it, moaning and groaning as I told him how much I liked his cock, how big it was, and how good his cum tasted.

He fingered me till I blew all over his hand, licking his fingers clean, and then inserting them into my mouth. I saw his erection start to slope back to normal state, much to my disappointment. I wasn't finished yet. I started stroking his pet, rubbing his balls, humming on his ball sack while I inserted a finger in his ass. He really got off on this; I knew just how to do it.

My husband entered the shower and they both fucked my holes till my cunt was enlarged and puffy. I gave both of them head in the shower, sucking the knobs of both, taking one turn at a time. I liked to tease sucking on John's 6 inches as I stared at my husband. He got jealous and grabbed my head, pulling me from John to make me latch onto his cock.

"Suck away you dirty princess," he said. I didn't mind, I had two black cocks on the go what more could I want? They both blew all over my back, the cum sticking to the wetness and curdling upon my back. I got out and dried most of it off me.

Juliana was standing at the door asking if I was finished. "Yes, hunny, I'm done. Where have you been? You should have been joining us," she starred at me with a smirk on her face, "Like hell you are finished. Only I can finish you off satisfied, baby."

She asked me to go down on all fours, as she fiddled with my strap on she had found. Entering my ass from behind, I was wet again it felt tight, uncomfortable at first, but once she started pounding my ass, I was screaming with joy. I begged the boys to put a cock in my mouth, I sucked away at my hubby's and I jerked off John.

We all ended up drenched in cum, covered in mixed juices. We were sticky and tired.

We never knew we'd become swinging lesbians and swinging fellas. I guess one night, one party, and couple of drinks can turn what you thought you didn't like into something your crave, ache for, something I didn't want to end.

We talked for a while afterwards, and we all agreed most defiantly it was the best fuck we'd ever had. None of us had fucked that many times in a row and none had actually felt as horny as they did. We have now made a pact; we've decided to skip the pool parties that arrive about every six months or so. Instead, we are just going to catch up at the pub, have a few scotch on the rocks and head to my place where the men swing their cocks in every direction and where us girls can't get enough of them.

4 NEVER TEASE YOUR NEIGHBORS

Shelly knew she had a good body, long curly brunette hair, and pouty lips that any man would want. She had a way with men. Every man wanted to get in her pants, but this wasn't as easy as everybody thought. Shelly was a dick tease; she was happy to tease but never really followed through with anything.

In her house were big bay windows. She deliberately would leave her curtains open for one reason: to tease the two horny fellas next door. She wasn't silly; she knew they watched her through each window. She knew they spied on her when she sunbathed near the pool. She loved it and played on it. Laying there in a revealing outfit, drinking cocktails, and sucking the straw like she had sexual fantasies on her mind. She knew how to work her mouth. Every guy that watched her eat anything on a stick did everything they could to get a blowjob from her.

If she decided to ask for payment, she would be swimming in cash. She'd have the customers piling up.

Shelly would act sexy with everything she did, even something as small as making coffee or wiping the bench. She knew she had the looks, and she was quite happy to flaunt it.

Two best friends, Jack and Tim, lived next door. They didn't really like the house or their neighbors on one side, but when they found out a hot chick lived on the other side who never worried about her curtains being left open, there was no way they were going to move out. They were not snoopy neighbors, but once they caught a glance of Shelly in front of her window with just a g-string, they couldn't stop looking out their window. From when they got home from work to when they were leaving for work, they were watching her most nights. They thought at first that she didn't know they were watching her. Of course, she did. They would get so horned up watching her not knowing it was all an act for them. She knew very well what they were doing. Shelly was a player, but perhaps she had teased the guys next door too much, and they were sick of the teasing. They wanted the real thing. Shelly was single. She found it hard to keep a boyfriend when she was always out flirting with other boys and inviting them to parties at her house. It was pretty late, around about ten at night. As usual, the fellas had their lights off sitting at their window just waiting for Shelly to do something sexy.

She knew they were watching when she saw their blinds were open and all the lights were switched off. That's when she took her body into business. Shelly entered the kitchen with only a bathrobe and a tube of her favorite body butter lotion, roses in musk. She lifted her leg high resting it on the kitchen bench. The guys noticed that she was flexible; they wondered how far she could spread. She squirted a little lotion onto her hands and slowly rubbed it in her skin, pulling her neck back in a sexy manner as she rubbed her skin.

Putting her leg down, she then lifted the other leg onto the bench and rubbed the cream in generously in an up and down motion like she was thinking about sex. The guys were already turned on by the time she was rubbing it onto her neck, pulling her hair back and massaging herself with her hands. She had long red nails and soft hands; she knew how to rub them over herself.

After she was finished playing with the cream, she then moved onto taking off the robe in front on the window viewing only a small black pair of shorts. She had no bra on but faced away so the guys couldn't see anything although they knew she was revealing everything.

They were getting horny, and all they could think about was fucking this hot chick from next door. It's every guys dream to screw the hot chick next door. After she had her fun, Shelly turned the lights off and hopped into bed. Noticing they had their window open, Shelly opened her bedroom window. She had a plan. She got her vibrating dildo out of her drawer, lubed it up and thought about having a play. She inserted it in gently letting the vibration pulse on her g-spot. She loved her dildo.

As she pushed the vibrator in and out, she moaned loudly, so the guys could hear her. "Fuck, she's playing with herself," Tim said now trying to push down his raging stiffy.

She groaned and moaned ever so loudly; she knew they would want this. After a while, she figured they would be hard enough. Turning off her dildo, she went to sleep. For satisfaction, the guys had to jerk themselves off, thanks to Shelly.

Shelly left for work early the next morning. When she returned home, she was surprised that it was windy, and so many leaves had fallen into the swimming pool. It wasn't her thing to clean up, so she had another plan. She would ask the boys next door to clean the leaves out while she flaunted herself around.

When she saw their car pull up in the driveway, she piled on some makeup and a revealing tank top. She walked on over knocking gently on their door.

Tim answered very surprised to see her at the door. He thought she looked even hotter face to face. He could feel himself growing hard, hoping she wouldn't notice. "I would like to ask for a favor. I need my pool cleaned out; would you be interested if I paid you two to do it?" Tim left her standing at the door while he went to find Jack. Begging Jack to say yes, they agreed to clean her pool for free. She was sly; she knew they wouldn't want her to pay. They arrived at her house a few minutes later with some gear to clean the pool out. She approached the door wearing a bathing suit on so small she may as well not bothered to wear anything. The guys were too busy starring at her rack to listen to what she was telling them. After she raised her voice a little, it got their attention and they headed for the pool edge to check out the mess. Shelly went and got a popsicle, and lay on her poolside chair watching the boys. The way she ate that icy pop was intense and extremely sexy. She rolled her tongue over the tip then pushed the whole thing down her throat. This girl knew how to tease. It took most of the next day to get that pool clean; the boys had a hard time trying to clean when she was pretty much giving her popsicle a blowjob. They imagined their cocks in her mouth and this nearly blew them away. After they had left, she tried to give them cash, but they refused; they didn't want her cash, they wanted her.

Nightfall came and she turned on all her lights. She made a cup of coffee with just a g-string and bra on. She didn't need any padding as her tits were huge. Just the type Tim loved sucking on. Shelly got bored of them watching her from their house so she decided to invite them over for tea. She planned to turn them on so bad they'd flirt with her. She didn't realize these boys were a little sick of teasing and they had their own plan for her and that teasing little pussy of hers.

Once again, she knocked on their door with just her robe on, stating she felt guilty for them not taking some money, so she decided to make them tea if they were interested.

Of course, they were. They showered as fast as possible, threw on some aftershave and knocked on her door. Shelly's perfume loomed over them; she had a scent they were dying to get close to. Everything about her was an aphrodisiac. She let them in, telling them to sit on the couch and make themselves at home. She followed behind them, and then walked in front of them as they sat down, letting her hair out of the ponytail and fall to her shoulders. She ran her fingers through it as she sat in between the two boys repeating herself, saying how much she appreciated the work for free situation.

Tim had thoughts. He really wanted to say, "Let me fuck you and we can call it even." He held his opinions back and kept them to himself.

Jack watched her closely as she said, "Gosh it's hot in here. I'll just take off my robe." They watched her drop the robe to the floor. Shelly looked at them, "Now that's better." It was for the boys too; it revealed more of her naked body. They needed to work together to get her to take off her bra and perhaps start sucking them off. She told them she had ordered pizza and it was about twenty minutes away. Taking another popsicle from the fridge, she sat in between them sucking on it as if it was one huge cock. Tim and Jack both hoping it was their cocks she was thinking about when she was doing that.

She rounded her tongue on the bottom of the stick and made sucking noises with her lips, a little of the juice ran down her chin. The guys were steaming; she was fucking this pop with her mouth. The doorbell rang, and it was obviously the pizza. She answered handing over her money and slamming the door. She put the pizza boxes on the table in front of Jack and Tim and walked away with that little strut she had. Next minute, they heard the shower going; did she just leave them there while she showers?

Tim turned to Jack, "Let's just go into the bathroom, bend her over, and start fucking her from behind." Tim explained she might claim sexual assault; they didn't know her very well yet. Tim didn't like Jack's comment.

"She's been teasing us for so long; that bitch wants to play games, then let's play too. By the way, think about it, it's not assault if she enjoys it." Jack laughed, in between words, "Well I guess once we shove our dicks in, she will be too busy having an orgasm to care." They still sat there.

Shelly returned with nothing but a towel. This was a little weird. She sat in between both boys and noticed they had hard-ons.

"Excuse me, what the hell." She spoke pointing at their rising crotches. Tim couldn't help himself.

"You can't tell me you don't want us. We watch you all the time; you're a teaser, so it's about time you got some real cock inside you."

Shelly looked surprised, as did Jack. He was surprised himself he had even said that. Shelly stood up turning to them both saying it was time they left, pointing at the door.

Jack said, "No, it's time we fucked you like the bitch you are."

Shelly looked angry at that comment. Tim stood in front of her and Jack stood on the other side, blocking her. Jack pushed her into Tim who already had his fingers ready to insert. Tim grabbed Shelly, placed her gently on the couch and pushed his fingers around her g-string and inside her. Her clit wasn't denying anything; it felt about to swell. It was obvious she was so fucking horny.

Jack kissed her, and with fingers inside, she couldn't help herself and kissed him back. Tim's fingers felt good inside her; they were a little rough, but it added a little more friction, which made the experience a whole lot better.

Tim pulled her hand down to feel his hard sword that was waiting for her. He pulsed inside her hand and knew she wanted it. Jack pulled his pants to his knees and pushed his cock out the side of his underwear shorts. It was stiff, long, and thick. He motioned for her to lick it; she hesitated until Tim's fingers drove in further.

Her moans became muffled as Jack's dick drilled strait in her mouth. He held her hair tight, pulling it closer to himself as she was forced to deep throat him. Her cunt was so wet it was dribbling. She knew she wanted it. Tim pulled his fingers out and made her lick them several times. Jack was close to blowing; he pulled her face close, pulled his cock out of her mouth and cummed all over her face. It ran down her cheek across her ear. Jack told her to open her mouth since she was a dirty girl and she needed to lick herself clean. She submitted. Her lips wanted to be gnawed at, pulled at, sucked and fucked. Tim removed his fingers; she was wet and her pussy was swelling up. It was begging for his cock. Tim got on his knees and pushed them into the couch, stabilizing himself as he pushed his cock hard into her. She moaned and felt a little uneasy as Jack got behind her and slapped her ass hard. He rubbed his dick hard against her ass cheeks, and she moaned as Tim fucked her hard, penetrating her deeply. She couldn't resist this.

Tim said in between sighs, "This is what you get for teasing horny cocks." She had nothing to say. She knew they were right. Jack fingered her knot, and she moaned even more loudly. Her cunt was drenched, and her knot was starting to swell also. Tim pulled out of that soaking cunt and let Jack have a turn at probing her pussy with his tongue. Her juices were running through his mouth and the taste was delightful. She had a hint of sweetness to the taste of her cum. Jack pulled at her lips. They were long and dark colored; he flicked them with the tips of his fingers before he shoved his cock hard in her again. She bounced forward on Jack's cock; he couldn't believe the tightness he felt. She was by far the tightest pussy his cock had been in. Tim shoved his cock into her mouth then pulled it out to slap her on the lips with it. Her moans now subdued as Tim had his cock in between her lips. He pushed in deep as he was about cum.

He felt hot, he felt himself pulsing. He wanted to fuck this pussy again and again. Both boys pulled out and made her bend over the kitchen bench where they could pound her pussy again, leaving it red and neglected. The bench was low enough that it got her in the perfect position. Cum dripped down her leg as Tim's load of nectar found its way out of that skin-tight, taut, purring pussycat. Tim knew how to make her purr fingering her knot as he pulsed his way in and out of her cunt.

Jack grasped her head and pushed her to the floor. He let her run her fingers and her tongue around where she roamed her mouth downhill. She dug his seven-inch cock far down her throat. His dick was big, sensational and smooth. With it down her throat, she was unable to stop the gaging reflex; his cum was soon traveling her tongue and running down her throat. His cum puddled on her tongue as she ran her tongue across her lips showing him the cum in her mouth.

Jack told her, "Your pussy is like a hot apple pie, moist and beautifully warm." He licked her body letting his tongue roam around her as he smelt her scent when she opened her legs. He dug his head deep and started to lick her out. His tongue was hard against her pussy, and she wasn't complaining; she grabbed his face and pushed him in closer. He fingered her and licked her, then fucked her with his hand. She was one wet bitch, and that cunt was something those two boys weren't leaving alone anytime soon.

She got up off the kitchen floor and strutted her ass to the bedroom where she got out her vibrator and asked Jack to fuck her with it while she gave Tim a hummer. She played with her pussy a little, tapping it, and slapping her pussy hood before removing her hand for Jack to enter. She grew wet before that dildo was even inside. The dildo was thick, and with her tight little pussy, it took some time getting it inside her. She moaned and cummed instantly; she couldn't resist this one.

That vibrating dildo was ploughed so hard in her pussy she struggled to get any moans out. She pushed her head into the pillow and started screaming in pleasure while it was penetrating her; the vibration was tensioning up her G-spot. She was dripping all over the bed; Tim was getting his ball sack hummed on, and he was in his own little world of orgasm. Shelly got louder and louder as the dildo got shoved in her cunt even harder as it was pushing against her pussy walls roughly. He slowly pulled it out right to the knob.

She expected him to pull it out, but instead, he rammed it in so hard she launched forward. He furiously shoved her with the rubber jackhammer as she sucked all over the other cock she had right where she wanted it. Before Tim could cum all over her, she pulled him down and sat on his cock as it popped up. Her pussy was so wet it slid in easily as she rode him on top like a bull. Her moves were like the rodeo as she pushed her ass up and down. Jack's pre-cum ran everywhere down his leg as he watched her movement; he couldn't believe she could move like this. It didn't take long for Tim. Usually, Jack doesn't like sloppy seconds, but the minute she was off Tim, Jack had her riding him. He didn't care that Tim's nectar was now on his cock because her pussy was a machine.

She rode him out of town and he came several times, yet she kept fucking, kept that movement going. Hot girl, eatable pussy, best tits and the fact she could move like this...Jack knew he wasn't finished with her yet. He motioned for her to backwards cowgirl, her ass was right in his face, he watched its movement as he slapped her ass red raw. He held her tits as her pussy crumbled onto his shaft. Everyone's cum was dripping everywhere; down her leg, onto his stomach, but fuck she was a good root. She rubbed her hand around the bottom of his cock and licked her fingers. So much cum all mixed together she was getting a little salty-sour taste, but it had a hint of her sweet nectar mixed in with it.

She climbed off, picking up her dildo and licking it clean. This bitch was hot as she was back to her teasing ways, pushing that silicone cock in and out of her mouth and slapping it on her cheek.

Tim handed her his cock, "Here's a real

cock, bitch, now fuck it with your mouth till its satisfied." She obeyed, fucking it deep, letting the precum drip down her cheeks. Jack came behind her and fingered her knotted part for a little while, then told her to bend over so he could take the mud track and fuck it like it was no one's business. Every hole on this poor girl had been fucked, sucked, hammered and abused. Her pussy was craving rest, but those two boys continued to use it. If that girl wanted to tease and be a bitch like that, she will pay for it with her pussy. Shelly had no control left. These guys were taking over and she had nothing to say about it, she knew it was useless.

Shelly pulled free from the men and went to make coffee. Tim followed, stating he would be the one to make her a coffee to say thank you for the fuck. She agreed to this, but she didn't know what lied in that innocent, nice gestured cup of coffee. She sat on the couch and didn't Tim jerking off and shooting it in her cup of coffee. Jack walked into the kitchen, smiled and walked over to where Shelly was sitting. He sat down beside, not able to get the smile off his face. Tim walked over with only a coffee for her. She thanked him ever so nicely with a kiss on the cheek. He watched her sip the coffee, commenting it was a little sour, but she would drink it.

After she had finished most of it, she looked in the bottom of the cup; the cum hadn't mixed in well. Once she realized what it was, she spat the remaining amount all over Tim. Jack grabbed her head and made her lick every bit of him clean. He pulled out his cock; she smiled saying,

"I got none on there."

"But you need punishment for that act of naughtiness."

She wrapped her lips around his shaft. He felt harder in her mouth, and he let go of her head as he cummed his load everywhere inside of her. She was filled with cum once again. Jack put his hand over her mouth and made her swallow every last drop of his pride. Shelly didn't learn by her mistake of dick teasing. She continued to do it, as she continued to get her tight little pussy pounded for misbehaving. Didn't her mother teach her it's mean to tease? Tim and Jack were never taught to punish for bad behavior but that little fur burger continued to be taught a lesson; she continued to be fucked, sucked drilled in every hole. Shelly was their cum catcher, a hot one at that. Tim and Jack returned several times a week, and they continued to cum in her coffee, making her drink it. She got used to it in the end. After several weeks, Shelly felt she couldn't get away from these guys and was so over them, so she moved. She continued doing what she always did, flirting with other boys and teasing the neighbors. She had moved several times after the neighbors started screwing her. She finally found a house she liked; she still undressed, walked around in G-strings and flirted with herself. She was unbelievable. Funny thing was, the house she decided to settle into had two fellows living together. That night, they knocked on her door, smiling and introducing themselves as Jack and Tim.

5 ONE WOMAN THREE HORNY MEN

The weekend was finally here. It was a warm Friday night, and I was feeling the urge to hit the town with a few girls. Kathy and Kim were married, but I was single so I was hoping to meet a nice fellow. I mingle a lot, with my blonde hair, blue eyes, and nice set of hoohoos. I don't have much of a problem. I attract the bad boys in my direction, which is perfect. The bad boys are the ones who know how to please a woman.

My phone was vibrating in my back pocket. No doubt it was Kathy. She usually texted me on a Friday saying the same thing, "drinks tonight"? There wasn't really a night that I would say no; once I chucked on some music and had a few drinks I was well into the mood.

I caught up with Kim in town about midday to get our hair done and pick out some skimpy clothing; the usual Friday. I found some knee-high boots and a black leather skirt I really wanted to buy. Kim laughed saying I'd look like a hooker. This made me want to buy them even more.

All I needed now was a top to go with it, something revealing to match my skimpy design.

I found the right one funny enough in the sex store where I also found candy underwear I so had to buy. Turning to Kim I said, "I wonder which guy will want to eat these off my ass?" We both laughed at that comment.

Kim usually wore normal formal wear. She didn't want to attract fellas as she had her own at home.

I got my hair straitened and eye brows waxed. After grabbing a coffee to go, we headed home. We had small talk at mine and then Kim headed home to have a nap before we went out.

I thought about doing the same, as we usually stayed out till all hours of the morning.

A few hours had passed and I'd slept for most of them; I felt groggy, so I started on the drinks. It was only 7 p.m. and we never went out till about ten or eleven, but I needed to get myself in the mood. I got dressed and fixed my hair a little and started on my make-up as the doorbell rang. "Hi Kathy babe come in."

She stood in the doorway looking me up and down, "You aren't really going dressed like that are you?"

"Well in fact, yes I am," I snickered at her. "What's wrong with it?" She looked me up and down again and said, "What's right with it?" "Well, I don't care what you think; I'm going out to find me some cock, so I need to wear revealing stuff," I said.

Walking back into the bathroom to finish my makeup, I heard Kathy in the fridge; she was already into the drinks. Kim had just arrived also making herself comfortable on my couch asking Kathy to bring her a drink.

Kim was the bossy one, Kathy was the flirty one, and I was the one with the sex brains, haha.

The night slipped on as we sat and talked about sex as we usually did. We were really a bunch of horny girls that loved cock; the best thing was I could experiment with different ones, but they had to continue with the same cock year after year.

It was ten to ten when we decided to leave. We called a taxi, it soon arrived and we were on our way.

The streets looked pretty packed; it was going to be a good night, I could feel it already.

We passed a few clubs that were rocking hard, and I had already found a few hotties along the way.

I did get whistled at from a few guys, but I also got filthy looks from the girls. Not that I cared.

I started dancing in the street and the music was already getting to me. I was also feeling a little tipsy so that meant it was time to find myself a boy. We went into a topless bar; these places were the best to find the good-looking guys, not to mention it got us attention being in a female stripper bar. Guys thought this was hot. I headed straight to the bar to get us three a drink, while the other girls found us a couch to relax on. I ordered three tequila sunrises in tall glasses with straws. A big muscled man was standing next to me. He handed over a fifty and said, "Excuse me miss, I'll pay for these." "Yes," I said under my breath. I'm in, and not to mention he was hot, hot, hot with really tight muscles.

I said thanks and headed over to the girls, still looking behind me to see if he was looking at my booty. Oh my god he totally was. After a few giggles with the girls, the topless chicks came on stage. Yes, we were straight, but we did find some enjoyment watching chicks strip. The other two girls were right out in front getting into it. I lagged back a bit until my drink was finished; otherwise, it would be all over me. I felt someone touch my shoulder, "Do you mind if I sit?" Again, oh my god, it was the guy from the bar; he just couldn't resist. "Of course not, make yourself at home," I said smiling. He placed his hand on my leg ever so gently. I looked at him, "Is this too much in making myself at home?" With him saying that, I couldn't deny I loved it and I was so fucking this guy tonight.

The girls turned around noticing I wasn't beside them. They just smiled and shook their heads that I had found a guy already. He shouted for more drinks, and by the time two hours had passed, I was very drunk. I was making out with this guy before I had even asked his name. "John Adams," he introduced himself as during kissing breaks. He tasted really sweet and his tongue felt really good.

He wasn't drinking; he offered us girls a ride in his car. Mind you, it was a Porsche! Like we said, we were quick out that door when we found that out.

Man, he knew how to handle a car. I hope he knew how to handle a girl's pussy because I was aiming for that. The two girls were so drunk they were yelling out to anyone and everyone, and while they were distracted, I rubbed John's leg with my hand and bit my lip in such a sexy way. He gave a little grin; he knew he wanted it. He had to stop at a friends place to drop something off and he left his cell phone in the car. I called my phone with it to get his number. I then waited for him to get back into the car before I sent him a text. "You know you want it," I wrote. He looked straight at me; how'd he know? He wrote back, "Hell yes."

I felt his lap; he had a hard cock, and rubbing the outside of his pants, I could feel it moving. He was horny. He took us back to his place. It was a mansion! He had a game room, a cinema room, and a huge diamond-shaped pool with sand and all. Without even asking, Kathy and Kim were half stripped and in his pool. "I'm so sorry," I apologized. He didn't seem annoyed, he just walked inside asking if I wanted a drink or something to eat. I was starving, but I didn't tell him this. He offered to cook hot dogs on a stick. I stood in the kitchen as he prepared the food. He lifted me up gently and sat me on the bench asking me to tell him about myself. I told him the basic stuff, blabbering on about nothing. He pulled my ass forward across the bench towards him; he played with my hair and kissed me, caressing my hair while he tongued my mouth. As we were deep in each other's mouth, his two best friends walked in whistling. He pulled away from me sticking a finger up at them and pulled me in for another kiss. As they walked outside, he said, "Don't you dare; they are both married." They walked back inside and turned the TV on.

John got the hot dogs organized; the girls got out of the pool, took one and got back in the pool with hot dogs, and all were smashed. I fiddled with the hot dog with my tongue, teasing John. He grinned as I sucked the top of the hot dog with my lips; I was a huge dick tease.

He went inside to bring me a glass of water, and one of his friends came out of nowhere and started kissing my cheek and my neck. I just sat there, and I was like, what the hell? He started kissing my lips, but I didn't move away. I kissed him back, and funny enough he didn't stop when he heard John coming. I pulled away to hear John say, "Hmm nice one Mark." They gave each other high fives as his other friend walked out and kissed me too. I kissed him back also, thinking this was a game.

John took my hand lightly asking if I wanted to go upstairs. I followed him, not knowing where his two friends had gone. I was drunk and didn't really care; I was getting a pork sword inside me, that was all that mattered. Walking into one of the bedrooms, I saw his two friends naked. "What's going on here?" I asked. "Well you wanted cock, you can't deny that, so we'll give you three."

I held a blank expression for a moment. Were they serious? Was I about to have sex with all three? Hell yeah I was! I stared at their swords; all three hard and pumping. I took off my jacket and tee shirt and let them drop to the floor, where I then leaned over to John and asked him to undo the buttons on my jeans. I glided my way out of them and slid over to the bed. I lay down, letting the two boys fiddle, one trying to get my g-string off and the other trying to find the clip for my bra. John came over and started kissing me; I was already starting to feel really warm. I could feel hands grabbing at my ass; arms grabbing at my sides; they all sooo wanted me. Who could deny them though? I was playing hard to get. I found out I was naked; I had lost my bra and my g-banger somewhere when they were fiddling with me. I felt a finger slide inside me; this was my weak point. I moaned loudly telling his fingers to fuck me good. I was kissing someone's nipples, not sure who they belonged, but so consumed with my orgasm to care. His fingers glided ever so freely inside me, touching my sensitive spot in a way no woman could handle. My cum covered his finger, feeling my pussy; I pushed another finger in. He let me ride his finger as I rocked back and forth. I was John's ball buddy, playing with his ball sack with my lips. He was smooth, and I just wanted that Jack-in–the-box right inside my mouth. Starting to lick his sucker, he made his cock pulse in my mouth. I focused on the knob where I ran the tip of my tongue over a little just to tease before I totally rammed the whole lot down my throat.

He grabbed my hair, and holding onto it, he pushed me back and forth. I was moaning to the rhythm of the fingers in my box as I sucked a hard cock down my throat. I tasted precum on the tip, pulling my mouth away and jerking him furiously until he cummed all over my neck and chest.

Without any noticed, I had a cock shoved in my ass; it felt tight, I was tight, but once he got good movement up, I begged for a cock in my honey pot. I had a hard cock in my ass plugging me fast with a cock being inserted into my pussy. I wanted to blow everywhere. I took the spare cock and started rubbing with my hands then sucking with my glossy lips. I rubbed my lip-gloss all over the cock and licked it clean, tasting his nectar floating with the strawberry gloss. I was getting the hell fucked out of me.

I felt a load eject into my ass, and as he pulled out, it ran out dripping down the back of my leg. The other fella had ejected his load into my box, then offered to lick me clean. I spread my legs like margarine and whined, groaned, growled as he pursued his tongue in deep.

He curled his tongue, letting it reach inside me further. "You like that, don't you little girl?" he whispered.

I couldn't answer. I had a thick round dick shoved roughly into my mouth. I teased it and flicked it with my tongue, and grabbed it tight in my hands. I slapped my cheek with it before placing it inside my warm moist mouth. I sucked hard as I was eaten out so well. I was happy with one cock but three?—speechless.

John pulled his mouth away from my burger and left the room. He soon returned with can of chocolate sauce. I stared at it excitedly as I sucked both cocks at once, taking turns rubbing their balls. John handed me the chocolate sauce saying, "Here beautiful, do your worst." I opened it and placed a little on each knob, lining them up. I sucked each cock one at a time: one was thick and round, another skinny but extra-long, and, as for John's, well let's just say, he's Godzilla and was my favorite.

Once they were close, I pulled away letting all three of them jerk their cocks hard until they all cummed in my open mouth. I was happy to catch their nectar.

I wondered where the two girls were. I

took a minute from sexual cravings and went to check, only just wrapped in a sheet. Both girls were lying in the sun passed out.

Walking back in the room, the three boys looked at me, and John said, "Bring that fur burger over here and let us fuck the shit out of it." I didn't hesitate. I was so wet, as John slid inside me from behind while I did a 69 with the other two boys. I love sex, especially getting head at the same time. Who could say no to that? I was drenched inside as I could feel my cum dripping out of me. I had help in cleaning up the mess. John wanted a break, so we headed downstairs to get a drink.

I ended up putting John's shirt on and jumping into the pool. The other two girls were knocked out, so they would sleep for hours. I laid on my back and paddled with my feet looking at the sky when I felt hands grab me and pull me under. John had a strong hold of me as he kissed me under the water.

As I came up for a breath, he started fingering me in the pool. It felt good letting the cool water enter me. My entrance was swelling, it wanted to be fucked, screwed, and drilled. It wanted to be taught a lesson. The other two boys brought us out a cocktail. I downed it, leaving only the cherry at the bottom. I took the cherry in my mouth with my tongue and slid it in and out of my mouth with my lips teasing the boy's erections.

I placed the cherry in between my thighs and rubbed it across my puffy lips offering some to each guy for a little taste. Each had a taste, and soon enough, I was getting drilled on the poolside by John and getting my ass fingered by another. The cool breeze created an erection on my nipples; I played with them a little before they were taken in Mark's mouth where he gently pulled at them with his teeth. It hurt a little but turned me on even more. I was moaning when Kathy walked in just starring. To my surprise instead of leaving and slamming the door, she took off her clothes saying, "How dare you have sex without inviting me?"

She was married, but I think as she started sucking John off, she didn't really care anymore. I pulled her face towards mine, and we started making out. I could taste cum on her tongue; it tasted yummy and I wanted some.

I grabbed John's sword, put it in my mouth and sucked harder and faster than Kathy did. I didn't like people outdoing me. I was a good dick sucker and I guaranteed I could do better. I played with his hole with my tongue and pulled furiously at his foreskin as he moaned louder. Kathy pulled my hair, telling me I was selfish bitch and I had been such a naughty girl. She was a mad bitch that shoved three fingers inside my box, letting my juices flow.

Mark left the room soon retuning with a few strawberries; he rubbed one over my tits then over the flaps of my box and fed it to Kathy. She was digging this, loving it as these guys were crazy horned up motherfuckers.

I bent over revealing my open lips asking who wanted to fuck me again and again. Kim walked over to me and said, "Bitch, spread those legs, I'm hungry." She caressed my thighs with her tongue and Kathy joined in to help. I felt Kathy and Kim's mouths inside me, and both tongues felt wet and smooth.

Kim let Kathy in further as she started biting my ass begging Mark to fuck her from behind. He got in close slapping my ass before he pounded Kathy with his 8 inches of heaven. Every time he pushed in penetrating her deep, she lurched forward penetrating me further. I screamed, "I'm going to cum! Who's going to be my cum bucket?" Kathy pushed Kim out of the way and got in first as I squirted my juice far, letting it run down her tits where John offered to lick her clean. I watched his tongue run over her nipples, over her tits and slide down her stomach like he was going for the honey pot. She spread open her legs ever so easy as he felt she was clean-shaven and was so suave to the touch. He teased her with his tongue; I leaned over and started kissing Kathy, letting my tongue run over her lips and inside her mouth. Her hands wandered over my body and I felt them pulling hard at my nipples and slap my pussy hood. Through mouthfuls of tonsil hockey, I told her she could enter my pussy and make it purr.

She grabbed Mark's hand and slid it inside me alongside her hand; it was a little different at first, but once the movement got going, I was far into erotic pleasure. It felt good, the two pushing inside me at different times I was still craving someone to fuck my ring thought. I looked at the third fella; he had been pretty quiet.

I signaled with my index finger for him to come over to me. He seemed hesitant but followed. I started rubbing his thin cock, getting it to throbbing point then guided it with my hand inside my knotted balloon. He soon got into rhythm and was pumping my ass hard as the two hands fucked my pussy with pleasure. John stood in front of me; licking my lips sucking my finger, I teased him. He grabbed my chin and pushed his cock in hard; I deep throated him for several minutes as I got the hell fucked out of me from behind. Taking his dick out, I gnawed at it gently then slapped it against my lips; I could feel him throbbing; he wasn't too far from blowing the load. I asked him, "Do you want me to spit or swallow?" He looked at Kathy and said, "Spit it inside her hot mutt letting it melt, then open her legs wide and clean her out." The cum filled my mouth; I held it in and got into position; I spat it inside Kathy and told Kim to finish it off. Kim obeyed; she knew better than to disagree. Kim lapped up the cum while Kathy still had her fingers inside me. I pulled away as I needed a breather from the scent of sex and cum.

I headed to the kitchen for some water where John followed right behind. He pinched my naked ass, and as I looked at the clock, it's now past midnight. John bent me over and pushed me on to the floor where he penetrated me from behind and drilled into my hard. Nectar started dripping down my leg and forming a small puddle on the floor. We sat in the lounge and chucked a hard-core porno DVD on. John instantly became hard when he saw the chick giving a guy a blowjob.

He pushed my head into his ball sack hard and said, "Suck away baby girl."

I did. I couldn't say no to that raging cock, those blue eyes and those tight muscles. Feeling intense pressure in my mouth, I gnawed down on his ball sack and took one in my mouth, sucking it hard then releasing it, picking up the other ball in my mouth and doing the same.

Kim walked in with a few red grapes; she pushed one inside my pussy and sucked it out with her mouth. She continued this for a few minutes. After having the grape in her mouth, she would pass it to John's mouth. I told her to stop doing that; I needed her to eat me out, I needed to her rescue my mutt, it needed mouth-to-mouth resuscitation from her. Eating me out for a long time, I soon cummed everywhere.

Kim didn't stop there; she continued to eat me out and let John finger her balloon knot hole while she pulled her front in front. Our hormones were raging. I slapped Kim's ass telling her she had been a bad girl. We could hear Kathy and the two boys fucking hard upstairs; they were giving that bed a good old rocking, not to mention Kathy's burger that would soon be swollen, numb and saturated with mixed cum.

We fucked so much that night. I loved guys that could go over and over while still inside you. These boys were fuck maniacs, and we were dirty little whores who wanted to play the game. We all headed out for a midnight swim as John turned the pool heating on. I wanted to fuck under the moonlight. I wanted to fuck John. I wanted Kathy to sit and watch me fuck like a troll whilst I watched her finger fuck her tight little pussy that was craving to join in.

This night was the best night we've had. I continued to sleep with other boys and go out with the two girls, but never did I sleep with boys alone again. Kathy and Kim are my close friends and my new fuck buddies. They were always invited to join in. After all, sharing is caring really, and after I had tasted Kathy, I couldn't get enough nor could I get enough cock.

6 SATISFACTION FROM A STRIPPER

The big tits and the pussies in your face, a strip club is every man's palace. Girls' dancing just in their underwear was what a friend and I planned to see this weekend.

It was a hot Friday, and we planned to travel to the best strippers that were two hours away. We got a friend to drive us down so we could drink most of the way down, which makes it more interesting. In the car headed to the boob shop, we downed a few beers before we had even left our hometown. We were in for a night we wouldn't forget. Cranking the music up, we chucked on some rap/hip hop and started dancing like total dicks. Two girls came ahead in the lane next to us; we yelled out, "Show us your tits." No chick ever did that when we said it. The blonde girl with the pretty eyes rolled her window down completely and pulled her top up revealing a gorgeous, huge, perked up rack, mind you she wasn't wearing a bra. I thought, wow, oh my god! This never happens. I think we all got an erection from that. The two girls laughed and we sat there commenting on which looked better. Both my friends wanted the brunette, but I wanted the blonde. There was something about her. No, I'm not the type to fall in love with any chick that notices me, but I liked her in some way.

The girls sped on ahead, and in our little bomb of a car that really wouldn't go over 80mph, we couldn't keep up. After switching lanes, overtaking, and waving to other people we lost them. I kind of felt a little disappointed.

We got a few blocks ahead, and looking out our left window trying to get pedestrians' attention, I heard a car beeping. I thought John must be sitting at a red light, but instead next to us was the blonde and brunette. The blonde looked at me and smiled, there was something in that smile, and a meaning I just didn't understand.

The two guys were screaming insults at the other people on the side of the road, so they didn't really notice. Jim was totally wasted in the back seat because he'd started drinking early. John was concentrating on the traffic lights, and she was trying to hand signal me something but I couldn't understand what she was saying. I was shaking my head she held her hand to her ear motioning a phone. Oh, she was giving me her phone number. I was excited. No one gave me their number. I suppose girls weren't very fond of red hair and no muscles. I was trying so hard to understand her signals, but I missed it, instead I signaled my number. She gave me thumbs up as the brunette stepped on the gas and they were gone.

I waited for several minutes but I didn't get a phone call. I guess she was just faking it, or maybe she was going to text me the reject line's number. I waited over an hour and then my phone went off. I got a text saying, "Hi cute boy in the car, I'm Jenny." I wrote back, "I'm Nath. I didn't think you were going to contact me..." Another message back, "Of course! I just didn't have any service in this area."

I was stuck what to write. Thinking for a minute, I wrote, "So why did you want to text me?" Her reply was, "There was something about you that attracted me. You seem nice." Straight after that message was another, "If you want to catch up later, I have work first but I can meet you afterwards." I only replied back,

"Ok, text me when you're not too busy."

The messages stopped there. John was asking who I was texting I just told him it was my mom, typical thing to do.

The rest of the way I couldn't think of anything else apart from that girl, Jenny. I wondered if she was one of those who says she'll catch up but I never hear from her again. This often happened to me. I think they only said that because they felt sorry for me and my red hair.

I pounded a few more beers as we neared our motel room. I dumped my stuff on the floor alongside John's. I stared at my phone the whole time the others were in the shower and fixing their hair up. They had the looks going for them, and they always seemed to pick up some pussy each night we went to the clubs.

I knew this girl wasn't going to text me back so I decided to let loose and just party hard. I had a few more drinks before I left, washed my face, and we headed out to get something to eat. I couldn't possibly drink alcohol on an empty stomach or I would be sick soon after. We had chicken Kiev's in a small restaurant and they were really good, but still I kept looking at my phone. We could hear the clubs and noise from the main street from a few blocks away. We were kind of tipsy; the alcohol was already starting to hit us.

When we finally got there, I can say the

club's atmosphere was fantastic. Everyone was partying and dancing to the special light effects and smoke machines. Mugs of beer were pretty cheap so we found ourselves having a few more drinks at the bar.

John didn't want to be in a normal club, he wanted tits and lap dances, so we went a few doors up to the strippers. Strip Heaven said the neon sign, and I couldn't wait. I had to always show my identity card, no security guards ever believed I was twenty-five. They always said I looked about seventeen.

The air hit me as soon as I walked in, it smelled like cocoa butter. The girls had to wear cocoa butter to moisturize their skin and create a nice glow. We all sat in a half circle couch in front of a girl on stage that was dancing on a pole. She smiled at our little group and blew us a kiss. John handed over a twenty dollar bill and she took off her bra. Instantly we all got a hard on, a bunch of hormonal raging horny guys.

We watched her, begging for her to take her G-string off and dance between us. "For a fifty I will," she said. Without hesitation, I handed it over, and she stepped down off the stage and motioned for us to follow her. We ended up in a private room; she pushed us one by one onto the couch and told us she wanted to tease us.

Shaking her boobs in front of our faces it felt good, she smelled good. We all got a go at flinging her G-string hard onto her skin. I had fantasized about doing this. She had her ass bent over in front of us, slowly pulling her G-string off. I was hard as a rock, she had a good ass from the back view, but we all wanted to see her pussy since that's the best part. Placing one leg on my knee and one on Jim's leg she was spreading her legs wide and ever so easy. She had short, good-looking pussy lips that were cleanly shaven.

She started to pull on her lips, opening her box for us all to see. We asked her to dirty dance on us, and she obeyed. Shaking her tight little pussy against our raging cocks was sending us crazy. She moved on us like she was fucking us, she was good at what she did.

After she had finished we asked her for a shower show. That was my favorite. "Give me a few minutes to have a break and it will cost you another fifty," she said. I popped it out of my wallet and brought another round of drinks.

We headed into the shower room and settled down in the bucket chairs with our beers.

Two minutes later she arrived, stripped off her bikini, threw it at us, and started the shower.

We could feel the steam filling us as she ran the water hot. Shaking the shaving cream bottle up, her tits were bouncing up and down everywhere. She squirted cream on her nipples and her pussy's hood then pressed herself against the clear shower glass wall. Her boobs looked excellent and I could see the cream starting to melt with the heat. She started patting her pussy with the top of the showerhead and held the water so it could run all over her slit. I could see she was sweating as she was rubbing herself against the glass wall acting like she was really horny. She was rolling her eyes in pleasure as she let the water run down to her pussy. She bent over and pressed her ass hard against the wall.

Seeing her pussy lips hard against the glass turned us nearly into the pre-cum stage. We were horny little fucks but we couldn't help it when there was a wet girl's cunt dancing in front of us and covered in shaving cream. I walked outside for a smoke. The night air was really cold. As I went to walk back inside so did another stripper. I let her in front and I didn't see her face, just her back view, which was gorgeous. She had real ghetto booty, a beautiful tan line, and long blonde hair. Well this girl I was getting more of a glimpse at. I tapped her on the shoulder and asked if us fellas could have a lap dance from her, and how much she charged. She turned saying "I'm only twenty, love," I nearly fell over. It wasn't because of her price that was really cheap for a gorgeous body like that; I nearly fell over because it was the girl from the car. She kind of looked at me the same way I was looking at her; I didn't know what to say I just looked away.

She put her hand on my arm and said, "For you I'll dance for free." I was a little surprised at her saying yes. I found the others shooting tequila at the bar. I told them I had found a girl willing to dance for free; of course they didn't believe me at first until she took my hand and led me into another private room similar to the first. As the others followed, she shut the door and locked it, leaving them standing outside the room complaining.

"What are you doing?" I asked her. "I want you to myself. Is that ok?"

By this point I had the hardest erection and uncontrolled nerves. I hadn't done this alone before.

There was something about her that made me feel I really didn't want to do it, but when she took off her bra I wasn't complaining. Her tits were brazenly exposed, very large and very uplifted. She had the darkest brown nipples I had seen, and they were very erect. She took off her underwear revealing her pussy. It was bare and perfectly shaped. Her lips were quite small with a little pink stud piercing that I found totally hot.

I was feeling stiff and was trying to stave it off since I was prone to cumming quickly. She placed her boobs over my face, rubbing them into my cheeks. She went a little further than most are supposed to. She stroked the crotch of my pants and kissed my cheek, leaving a small red lipstick stain. I was speechless, horny, and hard.

She walked out and I sat there thinking, fuck! I need to jerk off right now. Having another shot might help. Waiting in line at the bar, I asked for a tequila shot, and the barmaid smiled saying, "Free on the house for you from Jenny over there." Looking around I saw her sitting with another fella but smiling at me. Jenny. I like that name, but more importantly, I would like to screw her. A few of the strippers went for a break, and she was included, but she didn't hesitate to text me a sexy message after she left. "Hey hot stuff, want to hook up later?" Oh my god! Was she serious? I wrote back, "Sounds good." I'd have to wait and see. Later on we were pretty much wasted, and I was still horny, and not for any girl but Jenny.

Jim started chatting up a young girl at the bar who he had already brought several drinks for. He gave me a thumbs up meaning he was in with pussy tonight. Jack had already disappeared somewhere, so I guess he was getting a screw too. Pretty much drowning my sorrows, I took another two shots and decided to head outside clear my head a little.

I walked past a few strippers when I heard someone yelling out. I turned around and it was Jenny.

"Are you going? I looked everywhere inside for you," she said.

"No," I replied. "Just getting a little air."

She smiled that beautiful smile no other girl had given me before. "Look I'm heading home for a break. You're welcome to come if you like. I can get you something to eat."

I was excited. Was this going to lead to something? Was she planning on ripping my clothes off? I agreed. Her car was a few feet ahead, a nice red sports car. It was really nice inside, and I imagined fucking her across the backseat on the nice white vinyl. The thought was enticing, but would I have a chance of making it a reality?

Her house was just as nice as her car, and her couch was huge. I looked around as she got me a drink and even her bed was huge. I wondered if she had plans for us in that bed.

She handed me a drink telling me to loosen up and that I looked very worried. "I'll look after you. How about you? Let me ease those nerves." she teased.

While saying that, she started rubbing my shoulders. I already had a hard cock. She took my hand and placed it around her waist. She gently kissed me and then felt my erection. All I could think was shit I'm going to bang this girl.

She pushed me against the wall hard and kissed me furiously; she asked me to take her top off and untie her bra. They fell to the ground as I kissed her neck and fondled with her tits with my moist warm tongue. I was excited, energetic, and just wanted her to touch me more. I pushed her hand down to my crotch.

"I'm going to undo your buttons and fly. Any objections?" she whispered close to my ear.

"Go right ahead," I said.

Still kissing me and playing tonsil hockey, I let her unzip me. My pants fell to the ground, and I stepped out of them as she got down on her knees looking up at me with a huge grin on her face. She gripped her lips onto me and ran them down to the bottom of my shaft. Dragging her tongue to my knob, she sucked just the tip. Her mouth was sincere, moisturizing, and warm. I gripped her hair and gently rocked her head back and forth, as she deep throated my cock, and I moaned in pleasure.

I told her I was close to blowing while

she put her head back and pulled my dick with her hand. I felt she was ready to catch my load. I blew a full load with most landing in her mouth – a little ran down her chin and down her neck. She ran her tongue over her teeth and pulled her tongue in and out of her mouth, rolling the cum around in her mouth.

I groaned. It felt so good. She was good at blowjobs, but how good was she at riding my cock?

I lowered myself and pushed her onto the ground. I pushed her legs open and could already smell the scent of her wet pussy. I patted her puss for a few moments and leisurely stuck two fingers inside her. She was so warm inside and so moist. I could tell she was horny. I pulled my fingers in and out fast; I wanted to make her purr. She caressed the back of my neck, pushing my head in deeper and letting my tongue penetrate her with fury. She was really groaning now and begging me to keep going. She came several times, and her cum started sliding out her opening and running down her open thighs.

She was craving me, squirting all over my hands. I bet no one had made her this wet before.

She got up on all fours and pushed her ass in my face where my tongue rubbed her crack and hole. I inserted my pinkie finger into her asshole where she jerked forward unexpecting it. She started rocking back and forth pushing her ass against my hand.

"Fuck my finger you dirty little girl!" I sneered at her.

She pushed harder and rolled over, begging me to jump on top of her. I wanted it, she wanted it, and we both wanted to fuck each other's brains out. I complemented her on her pussy. It was very tight, shaved, and had a spicy scent. I captured her intense feelings. She was growling like a wild one as I pulsed hard on top of her. She screamed out that she was about to come, so I penetrated her harder and deeper, and soon her cum covered my cock. I pulled out of her and pushed my dick hard into her mouth making her taste my pre-cum, and her beautiful juices mixed together. She sucked as I fucked her mouth; then, sticking my cock in between her rack, I pounded her titties hard too. She opened her mouth to catch my cum as I drilled it hard into her tits. I throbbed more as I was getting close, and Jenny stuck a finger in my ass, and I could no longer hold it off. I squirted all over her tits and in her mouth. Jenny rubbed the cum all over her rack and all over her chest, and she continued to finger my ass with her other hand.

Afterward I was spent. She stood up and headed over to her bedside cupboard to put some classical music on, bending over and shaking her ass at me. She was teasing. I didn't like this. She was in trouble, and I was going to punish her in a way she wouldn't forget. I walked over and shoved my cock into her pussy hard and pounded that bitch strong.

She moaned and groaned, screaming, "Fuck me harder! I want to cum all over you!"

That I did. I exploded inside her but continued to keep on fucking her as cum was drooling out her drenched vagina. I grabbed her hips, got a good grip, and pulled her backward, thrusting her into me making her not forget my big ass dick.

I fucked and fucked her until her wet pussy was numb. I gave her a bit of a break only for a few minutes before I was back inside fucking her hotbox. Exploding again I moved my head inside her pussy's meat and started eating away once more. I couldn't get enough; she tasted just so good.

We traded places when she said she liked 69ers. She could suck me while I ate away at her. This was hot. I took a photo of her pussy and sent it to Jim. He wrote back saying, "Sweet, check this one out", and he sent a picture back of someone's fur burger. I just wrote, "He has a nice one ha-ha." I was always joking that he was gay.

She stuck her tongue in my ass crack and suckled away. I pulled at her clit lips with my teeth, gently sliding my tongue around and letting it wander around her pussy, spreading the cum everywhere. I moved to lie on my back. She sat on me and fucked me like she was riding a bull. She was drilling me hardcore and fuck, she knew how to do it. She chewed her bottom lip, giving me the look of innocence, which turned me on more. She jumped up and down on my hard cock as I helped her thrusting with my hands on her hips. I slapped her ass frantically as her pussy engulfed my cock that was beating her to her limits. She screamed my name as my cannon snapped at her harder. I flipped her over, and I jumped on top, slapping her in the face with my love handle before I inserted it into her sweet pussy.

"Fuck me! Take control!" she screamed in my face. I let her have me; I let her have me at my worse. Grabbing her neck, I took her body over. I planned to have it laying there whimpering when I was done with it. Her vulva swelled around my love muscle. It was enjoying every minute and not to mention Jenny. She didn't regret meeting me at the strip club, I can assure that.

She stood up, changed the CD over, and

started giving me a lap dance. I was very close to cumming everywhere as her pussy danced, rubbing itself along my shaft and over my knob, bending herself right forward so I was able to finger her vag while she danced on me. Struggling to hold it, my package blew its nectar all over her back, dripping down her spine and running into her crack where I made my cock rub it in.

She licked my growler clean, focusing on the knob and the balls. The motion in her tongue felt divine, and it would turn anyone into raging orgasms. The whole time I was with her, I never went soft. I was erect each time she touched me.

She went and showered while I rang Jim's phone to see what was happening. He bragged about this hot girl he had met at the strip club and how good of a fuck she was. Jack was the same. He'd got himself a load of pussy. They asked about me and I explained the whole story. Of course, they didn't believe me, and they thought the picture of her wet pussy was from a porno website. I told them I was going to have a rest to let the alcohol wear off but that was a lie; I was going to screw Jenny's kitty again and again. It was going to be sore after the poundings I had planned for it. I stroked my cock, telling him we were about to ride her again; seeing her naked in the shower fingering those puffy lips made my missile instantly grew hard.

She watched me start pulling my front man furiously as I gave her a sly look. She motioned with one finger in a very sexy style for me to come on in the shower. As I opened the door, I was greeted with her ass in my face. I slapped it hard several times and watched it turn red. I pushed my cock into her tight waxed cunt. I plunged her pussy like she wouldn't forget.

She moaned and ran her fingers through her hair. She was loving my cock, and she said she wanted it in her ass. Flicking it out of one hole, I then shoved it in the next hole. She nudged forward as it was a bit uncomfortable at first going in with the water, but after I started drilling her hard, she moistened up and soon was groaning to my rocking motion. Her legs were getting spread wide as I pounded that tight little asshole of hers.

After my cum had ended up all over the shower walls, I got out and got dressed. I called Jack and he met me down the end of the street. It took him awhile to find the place. I got in the car and bragged about last night as did he and Jim. I kept her number and I planned to visit her next time we came down here. I planned to fuck her silly again and again.

7 CREAM TO TINGLE, SAUCE TO LICK

I was craving pancakes with whipped cream and chocolate sauce - definitely my favorite. Mom asked me to run to the supermarket to grab some bits and pieces for the pancakes; I really couldn't be bothered, but I don't know, the sound of the word pancake sounded so good.

The walk there seemed to take ages. I have a car, but the sunshine was so nice and my body needed a good workout. The sun beamed down on the back of my black jacket, and it was beautiful.

My phone was vibrating in my back pocket, but I had ignored it. It was Jack from work. Jack has asked me out on several dates, kept calling, and sent me midnight messages. He is very attractive, and every girl wants him, but for some reason, I'm not attracted to him. In fact, I have slept with only one boy before, but I didn't enjoy it. This has been puzzling me for a long time.

I couldn't believe the store was pretty much vacant; no one was around, and this was good considering I don't like crowds. I took my time around the store as usual, as I like to look at everything and read my star signs in magazines. It's the typical thing of a nineteen year old. I felt hot in my black jacket, so before I kept on walking, I took it off and sat it in my basket, forgetting the top I have on was very low cut and showed my cleavage well.

As I turned, I ran into a girl about my age who nicely apologized for walking into me. I apologized too, and as I was walking away, I turned to notice her starring at my rack. Probably, she was just jealous, I thought, because my rack appeared to have more than she did.

When she noticed I had stopped and was looking at her, she didn't budge; she just kept on starring. I shook my head and walked down the next isle to check the mags out. After reading my star sign and walking towards the coke fridge, I noticed her in front of me, and strangely, all I noticed about her was her beautiful tight ass; she was wearing bike shorts, which framed her ass cheeks perfectly. "What the hell" I mumbled under my breath, she's a chick! Why the hell was I checking her ass out?

I was freaked out by this, so I left without my cream and chocolate sauce. As I walked past her through the exit, I heard the girl say, "See you tomorrow, I'll pop back in at one to pick it up."

I hurried home confused about what was wrong with me. I burst inside empty handed, mom staring at me puzzled. "Honey, where's the cream and chocolate sauce?" she asked. I thought quick, "The store was closing due to someone starting a fight." Mum was still asking questions when I told her I'd go back later. I never did.

The next morning, I awoke pretty late. I showered and headed downstairs for coffee. Mom had left for her Sunday errands. After having coffee, I noticed the time was twelve thirty. For some reason, all I could think about was that girl at the grocery store and her ass tight in those shorts. Without even doing my hair fancy as I usually did, I found myself soon walking through the grocery store door searching for her. It was a little past one o'clock as I got there; I hoped she hadn't left, but then, what was I going to do when I saw her? I looked frantically around, but not trying to look suspicious like I was stealing something.

After feeling a little disappointed by not seeing her, I decided to get the cream and chocolate sauce and get mom to make her famous pancakes.

So many options for chocolate sauce that I decided to go with the mint chocolate sauce and butter cream. As I was standing in the self-service line, a voice behind me asked what I needed cream and chocolate sauce for. Turning around, I stuttered, "Mom's pancakes." It was her smiling at me. "Nice," she replied.

I was surprised she was talking to me. As I went to take my bag, she slipped a piece of paper in my hand and walked away not looking back. I held the paper until I got out of the doorway, sat my bags down on the ground and read the words: "If you want me to show you what you can do with cream and chocolate sauce, add me on chat." Underneath was her chat address written in red pen.

Why would she want to add me on chat and what did she mean by showing me what she can do with cream and chocolate sauce? I hurried home and I loaded up the computer and added her email address, not sure why I agreed to do this, but still I did. Starting it up at first, she was offline.

Staring at the screen, I was running scenarios over in my head as to what I was going to say to her and why she wanted to talk to me.

I went for a coffee, bringing it upstairs and checking the screen if she was online. I noticed a small pop-up window in my task bar; she had started a conversation. Pulling it up on the screen, she had wrote, "Hey baby how are you?" I was puzzled that she wrote "baby" but I didn't question it. I just replied, "Good, thanks." She asked if had I used the cream and chocolate sauce. I explained I'd have to wait until mom got home to cook pancakes. Her next line was, "222 Malcolm Rd., bring your cream and sauce." I starred at the screen. Did she just give me her address? Was she inviting me over? Something inside me was urging me to go, feeling nervous I called a taxi and ended up at the address. A beautiful wooden door loomed in front of me. I rang the doorbell and saw her greet me at the door, wearing a tight outfit. I assumed that it was her nightwear, since it was quite revealing; perhaps, she was entertaining her boyfriend. These were my thoughts until she rubbed my arm in a very sensual way, motioning for me to come inside.

Entering, I could smell essential oils burning, and I could hear what sounded like classical music playing.

I walked in and seated myself on the couch. This girl walked over and sat beside me, handing me an alcoholic beverage stating it would help my nerves. I smiled and mumbled, "thanks," still confused why I was there.

Seeing her in that revealing outfit gave me a weird feeling inside. Was I attracted to her? No way! I'm straight. But was I? I hadn't exactly explored other options.

She took my hand introducing herself as Shelly, a hot name to go with her body. I finished my cocktail and watched Shelly move closer to me on the couch. I couldn't help but look at her boobs all tightly pushed together nicely rounded. Noticing me starring at her, she placed her hand gently above the knee, and with this action, I got up uncomfortably and walked to the other side of the room looking out the window starring out at the garden. I could hear Shelly's footsteps hover over me. I waited for her to touch me again, but she didn't; she just stood behind me. I turned to face her and I didn't realize how close she was. She looked me in the eyes asking if I knew why I was there. I just stated I didn't. She walked around me in circles, kind of dominating and really looking me up and down with a sneer.

"Are you telling me you felt nothing when you saw me in the supermarket?" She waited for my answer. I thought, "Felt"? What does she mean by this? Without even letting me start talking, she added, "So you don't think I'm hot in this sexy revealing body tamer? Because I think you're hot in those baggy pants and loose sweat shirt. But I think they would be better lying on the floor, don't you?" I couldn't move; I couldn't answer as she ran her hands deeply through my hair; it felt fantastic, and then she cupped my left cheek in her hand telling me how beautiful I was. I felt warm. Was I getting turned on by her? Impossible! I'm into guys. But then flirting with boys didn't feel good like this.

She grabbed my arm, pushed her lips into mine, and we started furiously making out. Her hands wandered from my neck, my tits, my ass, and then my clit, where she rubbed ever so gently.

I was horny, and I was about to have sex with a chick, now lesbian or whatever you call her.

She pushed and pulled at my pants, and soon enough, I felt them fall to my feet. I unzipped her jacket and was soon playing with her lips, gnawing at them gently as she asked me if I wanted her. I hesitated to answer until she told me we were alone. I then started caressing her tits and asked her, "Does that answer your question?"

I loved her smell, sweet musk vanilla, it was gorgeous just as her tits felt in my hands as I pushed them together and ran my tongue through her cleavage. Her skins quite tanned but ever so smooth, letting my hands run down to her clit and inside her pants; her pet also was smoothly shaven.

She slowly slid my tee off sucking my nipple as I helped her slide it over my head.

She whispered in my ear, "From that day in the supermarket, I have been playing with myself thinking of you". I followed her feet as she stepped a few feet backwards facing me in front of her mirror. I saw my hands on her; I saw her naked clit close to me; I never thought I'd say these four words to a girl, "Can I fuck you?" She pulled back, "Wow for someone nervous and hesitant you've surely changed the tune. How much do you want to fuck me?" Looking at her clit in the mirror I said, "I want to fuck that pussy till it's numb." With those words, she fully stripped revealing a tattoo along her back of two chicks kissing. It was spicy. Her body was very slim, slender, and very appealing, with no flaws upon her skin. My nipples entered her warm mouth as she dragged her tongue along each nipple then down to my belly button. I was feeling a little wet as Shelly rubbed her hands between my thighs. "Do you like me teasing?" she asked. "Hell yeah, but I can spread for you if you'd like to turn your teasing into hard-core pleasure. I can spread like melted chocolate for you." She pushed my legs apart and asked me to place one leg on her coffee table. I didn't disobey.

She ran her fingers down my pussy, playing with my clit lips. I begged her to fuck me with her finger. Pushing her satin fingers inside my warm pussy, she knew how to work with her hands. I cummed pretty much strait away.

She played with the hood of my clit with her tongue exploring the lips and sides of my pussy.

I asked her how I tasted. She said, "Spicy, like your pussy's on fire." Wow! She even knew how to dirty talk. "Do you want me to fuck your tight little pussy hard to teach it a lesson?"

I moaned louder as she slipped her fingers in even further. I soon once again squirted all over her fingers feeling it sticky inside me. She pinched my pussy grabbing and pulling it. She asked me to lie down on the fur rug in front of the couch. As I lay flat, Shelly laid on her stomach on the couch leaning her whole top body over the couch in perfect position, and she started eating me inside out. Cum dripped down my legs as Shelly licked it up, not leaving any to spare. I asked her to ride me like a bitch and show me that lesbian sex is hot steamy sex rather than straight sex.

She walked over to a small table with a side drawer pulling out a rubber cock; this bitch was crazy; she kept dildos in her lounge room. She handed it to me feeling it chilled, firm, and very smooth. "Put it inside you," she supposed. I teased her a little, rubbing the knob along the sides of my pussy. "You want me to shove it in; you want me to turn you on?" I let her lick the rubber cock before I shoved it inside my body-hugging pussy. I was captured I actually hadn't used one of these before. I moaned groaned telling shelly to grab the cock and fuck me with it.

I got up on all fours and pleaded her to fuck me like a dog. Doggy style penetrated deep begging her to let the vibration tickle my g-spot. She pushed, poked, reaching the spot I screamed, "Go harder fuck me with your cock." She got rougher shoving it in further listening to me moan, whine as I felt the ball sack hit hard against my ass. She started rubbing her clit along my ass cheeks while she pierced me narrow. She forced my legs to spread more while she pushed the dildo in, licking my very attractive ring hole I rocked backwards hard.

Stopping and pulling out, she grabbed my hand walking me upstairs; she told me she had a surprise for me. A king-sized bed pure white silk sheets and sex toys spread out on the bed.

I smiled and asked Shelly which one she was going to use on me first. "Any one you wish baby," she said. I moved my eyes towards the anal beads, black and white stripped with little pink indents in them. I hadn't used anal beads before; the thought actually was a little daunting until she used them. Shelly saw I was eyeing them off, "Oh you want to play with my beads?" She grabbed my leg, pulled hard putting me on my back as she crammed her index finger into my ass hole. It hurt at first, but with each insertion, it felt better. "Honey, I'm just loosening you up before we play with my beads."

After she has finished fucking my hole with her fingers, she slid her tongue in, creating a wet surface to insert the balls. She fondled with the balls inside her hands asking me to taste them, lick them make them wet before she implanted them.

She pushed each ball in slowly, one at a time; I twitched a little at first, but those inside me turned me on. She had pushed all the beads inside me; kissing my cheek, she asked me would I like her to suck them out of my ass one at a time. Fuck! I was horny I started moaning before she had even started. The feeling of her drawing them out with her mouth was unbelievable felling them pop out one at a time was a massive orgasm turner. She made the last ball be tugged out slowly I felt my pussy going wet again, I asked her to give me head.

She reached over to where her pink dildo was laying on the sheets and started gently whacking my pussy with it. She inserted the tip of the knob only a few centimeters in. This had me severely aroused as I pulled her on top of me, begging her furiously, telling her to fuck me, begging her to fuck me, ordering her to fuck me.

She left the room leaving me laying there horny as fuck, returning with a strap on. It was huge, over eight inches long. I pleaded with her to put it in. "Ride me like you're one cruel bitch, ride me like you're a dirty lesbian whore." She straddled herself on top of me forcefully inserting her rubber cock hard into my aroused drenched clit. She sat right up on top of me letting her hair out. Her blonde straightness fell past her shoulders, bouncing with her movement as she fucked my pussy hard. Bending down, she pursued to lick my nipples and stroke them with her tongue. She bent down further pushing her lips into mine I felt her tongue wander through my mouth as I kissed her back.

I was close to cumming as she pulled out, telling me to squirt in her mouth. Her head was lowered in front of my pussy, "Cum for me baby I'll catch." Just as she stuck her finger in my hot pussy, I squirted in her face. She moved back, wiping it from her face and running it over her hands asking me to lick her clean I obeyed again.

Starting to lick me out, she had good tongue action knew how to move it to make me wet. She knew the right way to eat pussy, that's for sure.

She sat in sitting position and asked if I wanted a break; instead, I asked her to get my cream and chocolate sauce she had asked me to bring. She hadn't even settled back down before I had the cream open, pouring it down her thighs and on the hood of her pussy. She starred at amazement as it spilled into her open pussy; she wasn't sure if I was definitely going to eat it out of her.

I slowly opened the chocolate sauce as I starred at her gnawing at my lip, giving her my let-me-eat-you-out-look. She started to spread her legs further without me having asking her; I guess she wanted it as much as I did. I ran my tongue from her thighs to her pussy, licking like a lap dog.

As I neared her clit lips with the chocolate sauce, she was already starting to cum. I rippled the sauce onto the melting cream and ate away. It tasted really sweet with her juices all mixed in together. She pushed my head in further, making my mouth penetrate her deeper. I sucked and licked as I stuck one finger in the nectar and feed it to her like she was a bad girl. We opted out for a rest. I laid back on the silk sheets they stuck to my body from the sweat. I heard shelly walk back up the stairs she had a whipped cream barrel in her hand. She pushed the trigger and cream sprouted everywhere.

Climbing on the bed, I watched her squirt cream on my nipples and belly button and then draw a heart around my pussy. Licking the cream gently around my nipples then dribbling the chocolate sauce down my chest, she told me to wait, not to move as she left the room. Returning with fresh strawberries, she rubbed around my pussy surely covering it in cream then running it up my chest around the chocolate sauce then feeding it to me.

My pussy was wet and sticky as she buried her head in it again, licking me clean so we could go have a cup of coffee. After she finished, we pashed most of the way down the stairs sharing all the left over juices in our mouths.

I got comfy on the kitchen chair as Shelly got us both our clothes. I sat on the bench just in her underwear while she waited for the coffee to brew. I walked over to her and asked her to spread her legs. I wanted to play with her pussy. "On the bench," I said. She looked a little disgusted. "Yep spread 'em," I replied. She smiled and opened her legs. I pulled her underwear to one side of her clit with my teeth, and instantly, I could smell her scent. She was very flexible, lifting one leg strait up as I eased my tongue around her pussy lips that were starting to become wet. I engaged two fingers in her tight pussy, and she started to moan, asking me to fuck her with the whipped cream can. Being thin and her pussy drenched in juice, it slid in easily, motioning back and forth.

She groaned like her pussy needed a pounding, which made me insert it further stretching that little pussy of hers. Soon, her juices filtered all over her and dripped on top the bench as I kept pounding her with the whipped cream barrel. She wiped the bench clean with her tee, and we decided to fuck outside in the garden. She placed the rubber dick on her, fastening it tight and bent me over the park bench and started fucking me in the garden. I tried not to moan; I tried not to say fuck me harder, but I couldn't bare it any longer; the harder she drilled me, the louder I moaned.

My clit was all wet, rubbing the juice all over my ass cheeks. Shelly pushed her pinkie finger into my ass and fondled with it while she screwed my pussy hard making me cum all over the grass. I pulled the cock out and pushed it into my ass telling her to fuck it like there's no tomorrow; she went crazy. She got rougher and rougher and I pushed back into her penetrating downwards. She pulled my hair into a ponytail kissing my neck, pulling hard at my hair asking was I sorry for misbehaving.

I moaned and acted like I was upset. This turned her on more that she pulled my ponytail harder as she let go of me with her other hand and rode me like I was a bull at the rodeo, and shit, she knew how to fuck someone hard.

After I was done, we laid down together on the grass, feeling a little prickly, but I wasn't bothered. Shelly ran her fingers down my chest, feeling that sticky cream and sauce. She asked if I enjoyed the screw; I knew I wanted more and I was not finished.

She French kissed me as passionately as we played with the lips of each other's pussy. Funny it took a supermarket trip and meeting a girl to figure out I was a lesbian. It was her ass in those tight pants that turned me on, but her pussy was even better. So warm and soft and easily led to cum. Her rack also was huge, and her tits were very well lifted. This bitch didn't need implants. I rolled onto her, placing my head in between her tits tweaking her nipples and running my hands down her thighs.

I asked her if she was interested in meeting up again, "You mean fuck buddies?" I nodded, that's exactly what I meant. Not having sex with this girl again would certainly drive me crazy. I rubbed her clit asking was I able to see her again soon. Looking at her watch, she saw it was just before dinner. She turned to me and she said, "How about we meet up in say about three hours? Let me get rid of mom for a few hours, clean myself up, and then you can pop back over."

Wow! In that short time? She must have really wanted me. "Um, sure that sounds good. I'll stop home, have a shower make up an excuse to mom and get a snack." She giggled and kissed my ear; she started nibbling on my ear lobe as she said not to worry about having something to eat. She took my hand placing it on her wet pussy, "I have everything you want to eat right here." I passionately kissed her and said, "I'll see you in a few hours."

I did return to her house that night, and we did fuck for at least three hours, and I can say she was a fucking fantastic fuck. We stayed fuck buddies for ages. We were both addicted to each other; I wanted her pussy as much as she wanted mine.

I just smiled when I saw her mom wiping the bench, vacuuming the stairs, sitting on the park bench, wiping over the washing machine knowing we fucked many times there mixing our juices together.

8 JUST CRAVING

My feet hit the pavement hard as I ran my morning fitness workout session. I had recently turned eighteen and would soon be approved to swim in the competitions, as well as my best friend Tania. We would be offered a great opportunity, and with our talent, we would be able to win gold.

Those were the words from our swimming coach Jack. He was in his late twenties, very good looking, very fit with excellent calves. He was an excellent coach; he'd always spend extra time with me and Tania. I knew it was because we always put in the effort. We'd always turn up for training sessions, and we always watched out diet, we didn't even drink unlike all the other girls. Usually, the swimming teachers go for the stuck up tarty girls that look hot hot in a swimming suit. Jack took his career seriously, and ours also; we wanted to be famous swimmers, and he was determined to help us.

We walked into the girls locker room where all the tarty girls were gossiping a bit before training, while Tania and I were eating a bag of dried fruit. Their bikinis were hugely revealing; ours were normal family suited ones.

We heard the whistle; Jack was ready for us. The other girls laughed at us as they ran pass.

They weren't even listening to Jack who was looking frustrated. Instead, they jumped into the pool and started ooling around splashing each other. Tania and I stood beside Jack waiting for his instructions as to where he wanted us to start. Jack smiled, "Of course you two girls are right where you should be". I smiled, "Always".

He flexed his muscled arms before pointing to the pool telling us to complete ten laps. The other girls did about four, but Tania and I did the full amount. It was pretty warm out in the sun which was good; it encouraged us to sunbathe. Jack was trying to get everyone's attention, but no one was really listening. He turned to us and said, "Off you go girls; go shower. You did really well. I want to talk to you before you leave though." We agreed and headed off to the showers. Before taking a shower, we did a few warm down stretches. We were out of the showers by the time the other girls got in, and they just sneered at us as they walked past us; this was the not unusual. Tania just rolled her eyes and continued to brush her hair. I was drying mine with the hairdryer before putting on moisturizer, then I headed out to find Jack.

Jack was sitting in the office writing some of his reports; I quietly knocked and opened the door. He smiled telling us to come in. "I wanted to talk to you girls together; I have reserved a spot at Tandy's tonight at 7 p.m. if you girls would like to go." Looking at my reaction, I asked why. "Well it's a thank you; you two girls always listen to what I say and always do right, so I'm treating you to a fancy dinner to say thank you... I'll pay." Walking out, I felt so excited; it was every girls dream to get a reservation at Tandy's; it was grand. Tania was jumping for joy, and we couldn't wait. We decided to get ready together, and seeing us always dressed normal, we decided to dress up a little and add makeup that we never wore. Most of the girls in the swimming club would pile on makeup, and then tell you not to splash them in case their makeup started running or their hair went frizzy. I had foundation and mascara on and I actually looked good. Tania had done her makeup; she too look gorgeous. We wore high-heeled shoes and mini shorts that were totally not us, but this was a once of a lifetime chance, and we were going to get noticed. We certainly couldn't go there in our normal clothes.

I stared at Tania, and we both squealed with excitement when we heard Jack beeping out the front. We left out the back door so mom wouldn't see what we were wearing; it was dark and Jack didn't really notice either. I sat in the front and Tania in the back; he opened the door for us when we arrived, and already, the atmosphere had caught us. It was fantastic and everyone eating inside was dolled up and looking great.

Jack looked at me and Tania up and down. We thought he didn't approve. When he smiled saying, "Wow I didn't realize how good your legs looked when you wore high heels." We just squeezed each other's hand tight out of excitement. We were seated at the back of the room in front of the open fireplace. It was just the best! I thought I noticed Jack staring at Tania's ass as she sat down, but maybe I was reading his expression wrong.

We ordered our food, and it took a while

for us to decide, as the menu was huge. I spotted Jack texting on his phone, and then my phone vibrated in my pocket. Did he just send me a message? He did have my number to contact me when training was on. I sat my phone in my lap and opened the text. It was from Jack saying I looked perfect in what I was wearing and I should have guys falling at my feet. I was surprised by this, so I wrote a several question marks and sent it back to him; I didn't really know what he was trying to get at.

He's reply read, "I would surely fall at your feet." I stared at my phone for a few seconds until Tania told me to stop being rude at the table. I excused myself and went to the toilet. I opened the message again reading it. I felt a little nervous as he was very attractive but a lot older than I am.

Soon enough, another message came through saying, "Did I offend you?" Of course, I wrote back:

"No, I just needed to freshen up."

"So do you like me telling you you're gorgeous?"

I couldn't help myself; I wrote back "Yes."

I walked back to the table staring at him; I actually wanted to lean over and kiss him, but no way! He's too old for me. Tania was staring at the fire, then she turned to me saying, "I'm going to order dessert, you want anything?" I said no, watching her leave Jack and I alone. I felt a hand on my leg; I faced him and he kissed me ever so gently. I didn't pull away because I didn't want him to, but in case Tania saw us. I felt his warm hand rubbing my leg. It felt good. He told me not to worry, it's ok. I felt a little uncomfortable when I felt his hand move to my inner thigh. Why did I have this feeling when, in fact, I wanted to fuck him? I wanted to screw my swimming teacher. I saw Tania's phone light up, and she read a text and walked to the toilet. I followed. She showed me the message; it was the same I had received. I showed her mine, and she asked did I feel attracted to him. I said yes. "You can have him sweet, go ahead." I wasn't holding back; I texted him saying, "Your place later?" The reply was, "Tania can come back too if she likes." I didn't want this; I wanted him to myself, but I agreed. We didn't even wait for her dessert; we left and headed to Jacks place. We sat on the couch with Jack in the middle watching a DVD. This isn't what I wanted... I wanted to touch him. I sent him a text: "Let's go upstairs you and me?" He replied, "Let's get friendlier right here, right now."

He started rubbing the front of Tania's shorts, then mine, and I could admit right then I was horny! OMG! Fuck I wanted him! Tania smiled at me behind Jacks' head. And I don't know what led us to do it, but we both leaned over Jacks' lap and kissed each other. Afterwards, we stared at each other; we didn't feel uncomfortable, and we felt horny! We moved closer, leaning hard against Jack, tonguing each other right in front of his face. I placed a hand on his pants, he was hard as a rock, and I was going to fuck that sword all night. Tania placed her hand upon mine and bit her lip as she rubbed her hand against mine. Jack was getting sweaty; I whispered in his ear, "You want to see me kiss her nipples?" All I got out of Jack was a nod. He was too horny to talk.

I took off Tania's shirt and untied her bra letting it fall into Jack's lap. He was horned up, as I started taking Tania's nipples in my mouth and fondled them with my tongue. Jack hadn't taken his eyes off us; we tongued each other as I felt Jacks hand on Tania's boobs. I undid his button and fly and slipped my hand down into his crotch. I felt his warm needle in my hand and I gripped it hard in my hand and slowly pulled it. Jack closed his eyes as Tania placed her tits in his mouth. I was feeling really hot; I wanted his pants off. I whispered in his ear to drop his pants, and he did immediately. The phone rang, he didn't budge.... we had him in a good position.

He was sitting with his cock high in the air, and I thought this was my chance to get exactly what I wanted. I pushed off my shorts and underwear and played with my pussy a little until I became wet. Tania helped me climb on board the train; I wanted his car inside my wet warm garage. He moaned with pleasure, rolling his eyes as I bounced up and down. I didn't want to go easy. I wanted to get straight to the point. I bounced harder as I let Tania kiss my ass cheeks; she was as hot as I was. I took Jacks hands and placed them above his head. I was taking control.

"Do you like my tight, young pussy fucking your hard cock? Do you Jack?" He moaned and nodded, "I want to blow inside you." I fucked him harder, while Tania sucked his ball sack. I felt an urge inside me as he ejaculated everywhere inside me.

I was hot, horny and I told Tania to lick me clean. As I climbed off John, he grabbed my hand, "She isn't really going to lick you out is she?" I smiled, "Hmm why not? She likes the taste of your cum among mine." John got hard really quick. "Fuck this is awesome!" he sneered at us.

I played across his lap as Tania moved my legs to rest upon my shoulder. My whole box was open for her view. Smiling, she teased me with her tongue before running it in and out of my pussy. It felt a little warm and really smooth I was going to cum anytime soon. I told her to insert a finger in above her tongue to reach my spot. She did and with this I cummed everywhere. She pulled her tongue out and passionately kissed me for a few seconds. She wanted to play dirty. Tania slid her finger wet with my nectar into Jacks mouth where he licked it clean, then furiously made out with her, spreading the cum over her lips and his.

I climbed back onto Jack in a backwards cowgirl position, pushing down into him hard as I could, a motion like I was riding a bull. Before he blew another load, I climbed off and let Tania finish him off. She sucked really slow and teased his pulsing knob as he cummed, missing her mouth and letting it dribble down her neck and onto her breasts. I cleaned her up and we realized what time it was, as we needed an early night for training in the morning. Jack didn't want to finish, but we were adamant we had to go. We got dressed and I kissed Jack so sweetly, and told him it's the innocent ones to watch out for.

We left, and when I got home, I sent him a message telling him I missed his cock.

We rocked up to training on time and we had a plan. The other girls were wasting time with the two lifeguards and I saw Jack standing near them shaking his head.

I walked up to Jack blushing and told him Tania had sprained her ankle and she needed help getting out of the car. He walked over with me, no one mentioning last night. Tania was on the far side of the car. Jack got and closed the door, as the wind was cold. He was trying to move her ankle when she giggled; he looked up at her as I jumped onto him and started kissing him. "We can't do this here," he mumbled. "Once we make you horny you'll do it anywhere." I pulled his dick out of his pants and started playing with it in my hands as I leaned over and kissed Tania. He was ripened and became hard, and no longer saying he didn't want to do it here. We fucked him several times and he blew multiple times inside us. I got out of the car feeling all sticky as did Tania. We headed over to the group and waited for Jack. He returned unable to look at us; he felt uncomfortable. He told the group he wasn't feeling well and training was cancelled. Not like anyone minded; everyone was happy. I walked over to Jack asking if he was ok. He just told us to go hit the locker rooms and get dressed. I held his hand, "Baby, let us help." He pulled away. "All we want to do is get hot and horny with you, don't you want us two young college girls begging for your cock?" I could see he was getting an erection, so I came closer to him whispering, "I think someone wants to come out and play."

Tania led the way, and I followed her into the locker room where we waited for Jack. We knew he couldn't resist. Soon enough, we heard Jack's footsteps in the locker room. He walked up to us stating this had to stop. "Well, two against one, we don't agree with that." I took his hand and placed in underneath my pants; I had already started feeling hot. He put two fingers inside me and made my pussy purr. Tania took his sword in her mouth and sucked away all his cum. He blew several times all over her. I went to the locker of the girl I hated most and wiped his cum all over her padlock.

Tania was blowing him again, and when he was close, she pointed his machine towards me, and we watched it shoot and hit my chest. We had fun playing with his cock and seeing who could catch the most cum in their mouth. He was a fucking machine, and we were his bad girls. I bent over telling him to fuck my anal hole.

Tania had already loosened it with her pinkie finger and lubed it all up with her tongue. It was easy access for Jack. He's cock was really red and thick. He wanted to fuck my knotted hole like he hadn't before. Tania guided him in as he rocked back and forth. I moaned my little heart out as his fingers reached under to my clit. He pulled at my clit lips and fiddled with my gooch using one hand; I pushed him far in, guiding him right to my g-spot. I moaned so loud he had to put a hand over my mouth in case someone was nearby using the pool. Tania stripped down naked and started licking me out. She was eating me like I was honey nectar. She pushed her tongue further into my honey pot as I felt Jack blow his load in my anal shaft. He pulled his cock out and motioned it towards Tania who licked it clean; he shoved it in her pussy. We two girls were dirty little fucks that just wanted to fuck and fuck his big muscled body.

Hmm, I loved getting raunchy with the swimming teacher. It was such a turn on to fuck someone so much older and so much more experienced. After that hot locker room session, the next day, Tania and I were addicted; we wanted his cock more, and so we went to his house. A young woman answered stating she was Jacks wife, asking who we were. Shit! He was married and still enjoyed fucking our little asses. "We're from the swimming team, and we needed Jack to check over our reports for tomorrow," I said.

We heard Jack's voice as he appeared in the doorway, shit scared to see us standing there. "Hi Jack! Was just wondering if you could check over our reports before tomorrow? They are in the car." Jack's wife smiled at us. "No worries," she said. "We can eat dinner later. I'll have a shower while I wait for you, take your time." Perfect, I said under my breath; we will certainly take our time rooting your husband…. Once we heard the water start, Jack stared at us; he looked angry. "You can't come to my house like this whenever you want, my wife will find out." "Please, just check our reports so we can go Jack." We gave him our cute innocent but fuck me now smile. This look he couldn't resist, and it gave him the largest erection quickly. He walked to the car with us; he knew we didn't need him to look over the reports, what a pile of bullshit that was. But still, he didn't resist. He followed us knowing what we were going to the car for. Oh well, at least his wife believed it.

I opened the door and Jack got into the passenger seat; Tania started rubbing his cock up and down as I sat in the driver's seat fiddling with his thighs. He was starting to sweat already but got the words out, "My wife might see; we better stop." He pulled away fast, looking disappointed though. He got out of the car and headed inside, and we followed. Did he really think we were going to give up that quick? He left the front door open; was this a hint? I knew it was. Come on in girls, fucking session in progress.

The water was still running; perfect chance for me to get Jack where we wanted him. I knew, as I lifted my skirt revealing my young ass that wasn't wearing any panties, this would grab his cock hard and I'd have him begging for me to fuck his cock. I especially did this for Jack. Tania started to finger my pussy; she knew the right spot to hit. Jack spoke quietly, "Oh my god I can't believe you're doing this in my lounge room," Jack said.

I pulled his pants to his knees and bent over their couch as I listened to the water still running. Jack pounded me hard in their lounge room as Tania pulled him out and started jerking him off with her hands. He blew all over the couch. He looked at his cum patch. "Fuck fuck fuck," he whispered I got a cushion and sat it over the patch.

"Now fuck me more," I sneered at him.

He fucked my ass hard but pulled out before he cummed everywhere. We started kissing each other; I was totally hot for my swimming teacher. Quickly, I pulled my skirt down, and Tania fixed her top and Jack's pants were back where they were. He quickly grabbed the folder sitting on the coffee table as his wife came down the stairs. "Ok, so you should be able to get those two markers in time if you two work together." He made up talk about swimming.

His wife offered us drink, and we didn't say no. As she walked into the kitchen, I leaned over and kissed Jack's cheek. She returned with drinks and I nearly fainted as we watched her sit on the cum patch. Right then, I think Jack's heart stopped. How was he going to get out of this one? I quickly got up stating, we got the information we needed and we better be heading home.

As we got to the door we heard his wife say, "Jack what the hell my pants are wet?" I laughed, but made it sound like I was coughing; Tania was out the door in fits of laughter. Jack went red saying the dog must have puked or peed on the couch. She shook her head but believed the story. We were really risky and that was the fun of it; we loved fucking John. We made regular visits to his house when it was his wife's shower time. She never did catch us.

We would watch pornos together and act them out, especially the movie where the guy inserts five grapes inside his neighbors pussy and asks her best friend to suck them out of her, one by one. We never did watch many movies; we were often too busy fucking each other. We were addicted to his cock. Jack knew how to insert anal beads in a perfect manner; he would suck them first to lube them up before inserting them into me and watching Tania pull on the string with her teeth letting them fall out one at a time. I was easily led to orgasms.

I asked Tania to fuck me with my dildo; the vibration gave off a sensation to my g-spot I cannot explain. It was the one thing that could make me cum over and over again in one session. I grew used to the vibration and always asked Jack to put a vibrating ring on the end of his cock before he knotted my ass. I knew how to use chocolate sauce on Tania; I'd let it slip and slide running down her warm pussy melting it quickly. Her juices tasted out of this world mixed with chocolate sauce, and I'd love to get a pile on it in my mouth and tongue kissing John letting it run through his mouth and over his lips. Tania then kissed him as I fuck her fanny with my fingers, inserting all three before resorting to inserting the chocolate cream sauce bottle. I would insert it a little, pull the trigger and let her pussy fill with it; this was hot. John would lick her up before returning home to give his wife a very passionate kiss. She used to comment that he tasted like chocolate. "Thank god for chocolate bars," he'd say.

We fucked in many places from that time after, more and more in risky spots like behind the library couch and in the parking lanes; we even gave him blowjobs at traffic lights. Jack can't say he doesn't have an exciting sex life. Tania and I continued a little bit of lesbian action on the side, but we didn't go too far together; that was saved for Jack. Mom always wondered why Tania and I never got boyfriends, but we went out all the time, always to meet up with Jack to let him fuck us silly. He was a bad boy who liked younger girls, and I can say we ended up hardly participating in swimming but got high marks and high awards, benefits of having a fuck buddy who is your swimming coach.

9 BLOWJOBS AND PAY RAISES

After I had divorced my husband and he took off to New York, I decided I couldn't live in the house any longer. It was too painful; there were too many memories. So I also took off heading down south.

I had always wanted to vacation there because of the big mansions and small towns so I packed most of my things and headed down that way. I wasn't sure where I was going but with half the settlement I had enough money to live for a while if I was unable to find a job strait away. Smelling the fresh pure air was heavenly, no vehicle fumes like the city; just fresh air and lots of land. I found my way to the local inn where I was welcomed very warmly. I introduced myself and explained a bit about my history, asking if there were any jobs around.

The barman showed me where the notice board was. There were a few help wanted ads for the likes of a handyman, a cook, a driver and a housemaid. The only one I really could do was the housemaid job. I rang the number on the bottom of the ad and was given an address to go to for an interview.

I showed up and was surprised to see a huge mansion. It was beautifully bricked with a huge water fountain out front. I stood and stared for a moment and was soon greeted by a lovely old man.

"You're here for the ad, are you not?" he said.

"Yes, that's me."

He introduced himself as Jack and he seemed like agenuinely nice fellow.

"Now before I show you around I'll explain the terms. It's a big house and the pay isn't very good, but you can stay in the upstairs area for free."

A roof over my head, some company and living in a house I'd always dreamed of. I would work hard for little pay; this seemed too good to be true.

I nodded in agreement and followed Jack inside. Stepping in the door I was hit with a musty smell.

"Most of the rooms aren't used. I mainly use the lounge with the fireplace, the kitchen and bathroom. I hardly use my bedroom as I often fall asleep on the couch."

I giggled. I could tell we were going to get along quite fine. He said I could go look around myself and let him know if I was interested or not. I was gone a little over an hour. This place was immense. There was a lot of dust everywhere; I could tell I was going to have my work cut out for me, but it was worth it if it worked out.

This was fantastic! I didn't even have to search for a place to stay. Jack said I could start tomorrow so I could get to know the village and look around to know my bearings first.

I offered to make him a cup of tea.

I found my way to the kitchen and found everything in there that I needed. I noticed big gold framed portraits along the staircase as I walked past. They looked so old. Placing Jack's cup of tea on the table I asked him about them. He seemed only too happy to tell me his history. I settled in front of the fire as he told me about his late wife who had died from a heart attack. He had no children.

Our conversation was going along so well until he made a comment, "If you're ever happy to offer an old fellow some personal gestures, I'd be happy to offer you a pay rise."

I sat silent. I was surprised. He didn't

seem the type.

I always said I would never do sexual acts for money, but I thought for a moment. He was an attractive old fellow and I suppose it wouldn't hurt to, at least until I got on my feet, but no I wasn't going to do that.

We didn't really talk during dinner; I guess we both felt awkward about what was said. Jack showered and retired to the lounge with his newspaper.

I went upstairs to look around more, I was a little nosy. There were so many rooms with so many antiques inside. It was amazing one old fellow had so much stuff. I headed into my room and started unpacking a few items and getting my night gown and slippers out I was going to bed early to so I could get a head start early in the morning. I had decided to check in on Jack before I went to bed.

I slowly opened the door. The fire was beautiful and the heat was quite intense. Jack had fallen asleep with his newspaper. I took the newspaper from him and folded it in half, placing it on the coffee table. I then quietly said to him that I was going to offer to help him climb into bed where it was more comfortable. Jack didn't budge, his skin feeling very hot when touched him. I proceeded to take off his cardigan as the fire was probably going to burn all night so the room would stay quite warm anyway.

I unbuttoned his cardigan and slowly pulled one arm out; he started waking up by the time I had the other arm out. He opened his eyes and it took him a minute to focus; I explained that I was cooling him down a little and he smiled. He let me lean him forward to pull the cardigan out. As I did he moved forward and kissed my cheek. I held my position for a minute I was quite shocked by this. Was it a thank you gesture or was he hoping to lead into something else?

Without worrying, I then let him kiss my lips and surprisingly I kissed him back. He was a lovely man and I guess everybody needs comfort sometimes, and without a wife or family he really had no one. With the niceness of letting me move in here and live for free, I guess I owed him. We passionately kissed for a few minutes as I felt his hand slide across my face. His hands were rough. I noticed he had the other hand resting in his pants. "Are you playing with yourself?" I asked. He didn't answer, he just took my hand, placing it down on the outside of his hands. I could feel his erection.

He asked to see my bra. I couldn't believe it, but there I was, stripping to show him my bra.

He had a nervous grin. I guess it may have just been awhile perhaps since his late wife had passed. He starred at my tits; nice young boobs that sat very well uplifted. I had a boob enlargement two years ago so they were in good shape.

He asked me to pull my pants down and show him my backside. I did this and I could tell he liked very much. I revealed my tattoo just above my pussy's hood, which he asked if he could touch. He ran his finger around the outline. This was quite a turn on. Wow, I was getting turned on by an older man and I could tell that the way this was going we would end up fucking by the time the night was out. He poked his fingers further down near my pussy feeling the line of my G-string. He started playing around, fiddling and fondling with my now warm cunt. I kissed his neck as he found the slit of my pussy.

Pulling lightly on my lips and rubbing his fingers over the slit, I told him he could insert his fingers if he wanted to. I felt over his pants, and then pushed my hands under his pants and underwear. His cock was very hard and by feeling it, I could tell it was big a lot bigger than what I had in the past. It was going to feel amazing inside my pussy. His callused hands slid inside me and he told me I was a bad girl and I needed to be punished.

The roughness of his hands felt so good inside me as he pushed in and out. Licking his finger, he told me I tasted sweet.

My pussy started throbbing; it wanted his hands inside again. I loved it. I pulled his shirt off and pulled his singlet over his head, reaching for his nipples with my mouth. His chest was hairy. I started kissing, licking, tenderizing his nipples till they were starting to get erect. Jack continued to shove his fingers inside and outside of me. Jack stood up and I ordered him to take his bottoms off; he obeyed.

His cock popped out of his pants and was begging for my lips to clutch it tight. I told Jack to remain standing as I dragged my tongue across his shaft. I hummed on his ball sack as he moaned with pleasure, gliding his dick inside my mouth.

I started feeling wet myself as a little pre-cum stained my tongue. I looked up into his eyes. They were closed, and he was horny and full of enjoyment. I placed his dick in my hand and flapped it against my tongue gnawing at my lips as I felt him get harder. "Be a good girl and swallow for me," he said. I fucked his cock in my mouth, sucking his knob only a few inches inside of my mouth. I fondled his cock hole with my tongue as I felt my mouth fill with his creamy nectar. It tasted salty and it dripped out my mouth; it was a full load.

I swallowed his load in one mouthful and felt his fingers enter me from behind. My pussy was craving him. I wanted to fuck this old man, and give him the ride of his life. I wanted an old man to make me cum.

I bent down in front of him and shook my ass furiously. He slapped it hard after I asked him to fuck me. "I'll fuck the youth out of you girl. I'll have you cumming."

I wanted him bad now. I moved back onto his cock, rubbing my ass cheeks up and down, teasing his erection. He moved in close, grabbing his cock and roughly jolting it inside my wet cunt. He thrust into me. He talked dirty to me as he slapped my ass telling me to take it like I've misbehaved.

"Fuck, your old cock feels good inside me!" I got those words out between moans. "Harder, faster".

I yelled his name and he penetrated me deeper as I moved down further.

He fucked me like a dog. I craved his cock. My pussy throbbed for it.

He pulled out after he blew his load inside me, for then I started licking him clean and tasting him cum. I felt him reach down to grab my legs and push my legs out. They spread ever so easy for him. He licked over my pussy hood and I forced his head inside. He tasted our cum mixed together with his warm saliva.

He knew how to work his tongue; he curled it and pushed in further. I was close to cumming everywhere.

Licking his lips, he rubbed my ass with his cock slapping it against my side. Jack pulled me up and threw me over his lap and started fingering my ass. I was tight and it hurt a little, but it got easier as my asshole started lubricating up. He threw me back on the floor and started dry humping me; I moaned a little he started rubbing my pussy. His cock was hard again. I could tell it was inviting me to play. I licked the knob a few times before I was jerking him off real hard, I wanted it inside me. My pussy was throbbing, and it wanted to be fucked. Instead he pushed his penis hard into my ass, and I begged him to spread his nectar inside me. I captured his balls in my hands and rubbed so vigorously. I was in love with an old man's cock. He pulled his cock out and slammed it against my wet slit then shoved it back in my ass. He banged it hard and I groaned as loud as I could. He panted and fucked hard, pulling out, blowing all over my back and ass cheeks.

I sat on his armchair and opened my legs revealing my tight pussy that was becoming really wet. He dug his mouth inside as my own cum lined his tongue with a honeyed taste.

I felt dizzy as I was close to an orgasm. He pulled his tongue out as I squirted everywhere. There was a knock at the door. Jack called out, "Hang on a minute," as he shoved his cock hard inside me and thrust fast until he had cum inside me again, and I was drenched. He put on his shirt and pants and headed to answer the door. I ran upstairs to shower and put on clean clothes.

A minute later I heard Jack call out saying he was going for a walk with the dogs through the forest. Jack had acres of forest around his house; it was pure beauty really.

I called out and acknowledged I had heard him. He said I was welcome to join him a little bit later on.

I turned the coffee machine on and the freshly steamed beans smelt divine. I took my coffee and headed outside. I sat in the garden for a few minutes to enjoy the fresh breeze. Finishing my coffee, I headed down to try and find Jack. I wanted to talk about what had happened.

Green grass, thick logs and luscious trees; the forest was perfect. About twenty minutes into the forest I could hear Jack's three dogs barking. Walking through I found a large dam that the dogs were swimming in. I searched nearby looking for Jack. To my surprise, Jack was laying on a picnic rug naked. I laughed, "What are you doing?" "I own this land, just me and you out here. Do you want to fuck out in nature?" I was a bit skeptical about this. Someone might see, but it was interesting. I had never screwed in a forest before. I bent down next to him and kissed his hand.

"How much do you want to fuck my tight little pussy?" "Much like you're my little whore," he quietly said. I placed his hands on my rack and he massaged them for a few seconds before pushing his hand down my top, undoing my bra and groping my tits. I bent down and licked his cock and it tasted so good. I started sucking wildly, the idea of him unloading himself inside my mouth made me hot and steamy. I shoved his cock further down my throat; he loved to be deep throated. He was pulling my pussy lips. Grabbing my hips Jack rammed my ass into the front of him; I reached under and helped push his cock into my pussy.

He was riding me hard. I thrust myself back and forth into him, helping his shaft insert further. I wanted to keep fucking this old man over and over. Pleasure was filling me. He held my hips and pushed harder, then he exploded his nectar everywhere inside me.

I pulled his cock out of my cunt and jumped on top of him. I wanted to dominate, and I wanted to take control. I was the boss and it was about time he understood this.

I sat upright on his pussy juice soaked cock and drove into it harder. I fucked and fucked, moaning, groaning, drilled and screwed. His hands grabbed my ass hard. He pulled my ass cheeks up and slapped them hard. I sucked his tongue, sucked his ear lobe, fondled with his nipples till they were erect with my tongue. I spat on his nipples and licked it up again. He was moaning, a horny fucked old man loving some younger pussy. He pleaded with me to fuck him harder, to fuck him like he'd never forget. He started yelling my name; I replied, "Oh Jack, I love fucking your cock." He pinched my nipples as he blew inside me.

I could feel the warm cum run out of me, but I fucked him more. My cum and his cum mixed together, running onto his stomach. His cock was wet, drenched, soaked but I wasn't letting him out yet. He gently fingered my ass as I told him my pussy needed to be taught a lesson. Jack pushed me off getting on top of me, taking control. I felt a big cum soaked spot underneath my ass but we kept on screwing. The phone rang. Jack got off me, leaning over he answered. While he was talking on the phone I thought about cleaning myself up a little, perhaps getting a towel to soak up some of the mess. This thought seemed to leave my mind straight away as I started sucking him off again. He was trying to focus on the phone call, trying hard not to moan or groan.

I licked up and down his shaft, I sucked his balls, got them in my mouth and gently pulled. I grabbed the bottom of his cock and started pulling hard as I stuck my mouth on the end of his knob and lapped away. He was closing his eyes and putting his head up in the air in pleasure. I sucked quickly and deep throated him and he was panting, unable to take it anymore. He put the phone down, moaned extremely loud and blew a load everywhere in my mouth. It starting sliding down my throat and dripped out the side of my mouth.

I'm sure he had no cum left; he had emptied every bit of sperm somewhere inside me. I said to him that we should take a rest, and Jack soon fell asleep beside me. I headed to the bathroom and cleaned myself up, as I felt wet and sticky. I was tired but didn't feel like sleeping. I still felt a little bit horny.

Flopping onto my bed, my fingers

somehow made it to my pussy where I started playing with myself for a bit trying to help the urge go away. I was reaching my level and I realized as I let the cum flow Jack was standing at the door watching me.

"So this is what you do in your spare time, is it?" "Yes, when there isn't anyone around to do it for me," I said. Jack walked in and smelled my pussy, then stuck two fingers in and started moving them in and out. I opened my legs further and told Jack just where my vibrator was. Pulling his fingers out, he leaned over to my top drawer and pulled my rubber cock out. Slapping my face with it, slapping my pussy hood, I begged him to shove it in my wet cunt.

He only placed about two inches of the knob in and turned the vibration on. I came immediately, over and over. My poor favorite cock was soaking wet. Jack took it out and slapped my pussy hard, again letting his cum drip from my vagina. It was indecent but I loved it as he worked it hard, and I moved my hips hard. I wanted it harder, faster. I was a slut for Jack; he was my personal fucker on demand.

He bent me over the bed and ever so gently pushed my dildo in my ass. It hurt stretching but with my juices all over it, it soon worked up real good. I was moaning but it still wasn't as good as being in my pussy. I lowered myself further down and Jack fucked harder, he was lasting long this time. He threw my dildo to the other side of the room and said "I'll show you a real cock; I'll show you I can screw you harder than any dildo". He did.

He cock was erect inside me, I could feel it. I didn't want him to cum in me, I wanted him to cum all over me.

I got back on the bed and pushed my boobs together asking him to blow all over my tits.

I pulled him out and grabbed his hips motioning for him to come up further to my chest. He placed his cock nicely in between my cleavage and fucked away. It felt good; I took my left hand and started playing with my pussy while he fucked my tits. He pushed his cock in my mouth as I sucked for a few seconds he put it back in between my boobs and started pounding again. I really wanted to suck his balls; he didn't mind, he did as I asked. I towed them with my lips and tickled with my tongue this turned him on more. I felt dirty; he was a lot older than me but very experienced. I could tell I wasn't going to be fucking anyone my age anymore. He knew how I liked it and I knew he loved the younger pussy.

He pushed hard and exploded his load all over my tits, all down my neck, soaking the area in which I laid. Leaning down,

Jack kissed me for a few minutes asking if I was happy fucking an old man. "I never thought I would say it, but fuck you're good!" He laughed and said every woman who fucks him must make him a sandwich afterwards. I smiled and spread my legs telling him to eat my pussy. He licked, sucked and fucked with his tongue; he had good motion. I ran my hands across his face, in his hair, then I held his head tight as he spat in my pussy and licked it up again.

"You like it dirty don't you?" he yelled at me as he started spanking my ass again. "Fuck, you're a whore, a dirty little whore." I blew all over his face. I wanted Jack to fuck my boobs, pressing them hard together. I told him to fuck them and cum all over my chest. He fucked my cleavage hard as he slipped a finger into my ass and fiddled inside. I was horny, my pussy was growing wet again and it started to swell.

His finger felt good inside my ass but not as good as in my pussy. I used one of my hands to play with his balls and used my mouth to just lick the tip of his cock with my tongue as each time he pushed forward. I was cumming a great deal and wanted one last fuck. Jack agreed, sticking his cock in straight away. He felt real wet, sperm still covering his end. I whimpered that it was really good, and he banged my poor little pussy really rough; I could feel myself starting to swell. I had already cum several times and I begged him to blow inside me. He told me he was close, and I told him to pound hard. Instead he pulled out, got off the bed and walked out of the room.

"What, you can't leave me like this!"

"Yes I can," he replied, "It's then that I know you'll be back for more."

From the hallway he called "Fuck, you have most certainly earned yourself a pay rise!"

10 STRANGER ON A TRAIN

I awoke at early dawn to see the sun beaming through my bedroom window. My husband had already left for work at around 7am. I looked at the clock; I slept till 9am. It was a beautiful day outside. I headed downstairs in my see-through black silk gown. I craved coffee. The brewing coffee filled the kitchen with a heavenly aroma.

I heard a knock at the front door. I was embarrassed to still be in my night gown. I didn't want to answer, so instead I peeked out behind the curtain. Strangely enough there was no one there. Perhaps this was a prank, but looking down at my feet, just sticking out from the table under the window was a blank white envelope. It was not addressed to anyone. Someone must have pushed it through the mail slot. Pushing an errant strand of black hair off of my face, I felt puzzled but wanted to read this immediately. Placing the envelope on the table, I stared at it for a few minutes. Serving myself some coffee, I sat down, eager to open it. Reading over those few words made me feel sick:

"Do you know your husband's fully qualified at fucking the girl next door?"

Shocked by this, I read the few words over and over. Hoping I'd misread it, but no, it said what it said. The girl next door, Suzie, was a cute girl, quite young, only in her early twenties. I, on the other hand, was thirty five years of age. She was a pretty girl with gorgeous long blonde hair she usually kept in a low ponytail. She has a very slender body and has perfect skin. She is very fashionable and loves high heels, and yes, she knew how to wear them. She often brought over new food recipes for me to try and often gave me a few freshly picked roses.

"Of course not!" I spoke out loud. She wouldn't be involved in screwing sessions with my husband. We were good friends, but then, I thought, friends aren't always true friends. Perhaps she was my husband's friend. Maybe they were friends with benefits. This was widely heard of.

Staring at the letter, I thought maybe she had written this as a joke or maybe as her way of telling me what was going on. Perhaps she felt a little guilty, or maybe she wanted to be a smart bitch.

I love my husband, but if he was fucking the girl next door, then I could play that game.

First, I needed to find out if these words were true. I rang Suzie. She answered politely.

"Hello, Suzie here."

"Hey Suz, was wondering. I'm heading out with a friend tonight for a few drinks and a girls' movie night. Jack isn't feeling too well, so would you mind popping over a bit later on to check on him? Around 10pm. I'm leaving around 9pm."

"Of course. Sure, I'd be happy to."

After saying thanks and goodbye, I hung up.

"I'm sure you'll be happy to, but you forgot to mention you're happy to fuck my husband, you cow."

I said this out loud and then thought, "I must be careful; this may just be a prank." Innocent until proven guilty is the motto.

I rang my husband being my normal self and told him I planned a night out with the girls. He was more than happy, sounding as if he was pleading with me to go, but in a roundabout way.

The day raced by, and after attending to the housework and staring at the letter for several hours, I left the house. I walked outside and positioned myself in a hole in between the two hedges. I was cold; I had to know. I planned to catch them red-handed, and by the tone of both voices, something was going on.

Soon after my husband's headlights blinded me, I watched him walk inside and call someone on his mobile. I had a perfect view of the lounge and bedroom I was sure to catch him. He was on the phone for several seconds before heading upstairs for a shower. This was unlike him. He always showered in the night, right before bed.

It soon reached 10pm. Right on the minute, Suzie walked over the front garden and knocked several times on the door. She was dressed in a leather miniskirt and a very revealing tank top. There was no answer, so she opened the door and yelled out. Jack came down in a towel greeting her. I could just hear what they were saying: Jack apologized for being in a towel. I was waiting for her to rip the towel off his naked ass, but instead, she said, "I was just checking if you needed anything while Jill was with the girls." Jack smiled and said, "No, thanks." He then said goodbye and shut the door. What the hell? He didn't even look at her boobs half hanging out, or her legs, or any part of her sexy figure. Perhaps this was a prank. I felt relieved. I was horribly wrong.

I was just sighing with relief when I could hear what sounded like high heels approaching the house. Suzie was back; maybe she was just checking to see if I had left.

At the door stood a tall woman dressed in black with a hood. I couldn't see her face.

I dry retched when I heard the voice; surely it couldn't be. I watched in contempt as Jack started kissing her; she hadn't even got through the doorway. She took her coat off and revealed my worst nightmare. I watched her kiss his neck, and I watched him slide his fingers up her skirt; she was moaning while I was fuming. Fuck that bastard, fuck that whore. It was my sister. She had moved next door when our mother died so we could keep close. I didn't even think of her. I had blamed Suzie. I looked away. How could she do this? How could he? Looking back in the window, I saw that she was sucking his cock in the hallway leaning against the portrait of me. I needed to look away. I wanted to run, but where? I couldn't drive; my keys were inside the house. Confused and angry, I just got up and ran. I didn't look back. I stopped at the train. I didn't know where I was going, but anywhere was better than this town. The next train was coming in fifteen minutes. I sat on the bench thinking about what I saw, and then I thought: if it were Suzie, it would have been alright, but my sister?! I hated that prick.

I started crying uncontrollably when the train rolled up. Realising that I had no money on me and all my personal belongings were in the car and the keys were at home, I sobbed even louder. A young man approached me. Looking at him, I yelled in his face, "I'm not interested in what you're selling or whatever it is you're wanting." He sat down beside me stating he was selling his friendship for free if I was interested. I thought, "Wow, a guy trying to get into my pants." He thought I was vulnerable because I was upset. I didn't look at him; he got the hint and stood up, placing a pile of money in my lap. This aggravated me. I yelled loudly: "You think I'm a whore?" He laughed at this statement. "No," he replied. "I noticed you don't have a handbag and you're crying, so something obviously happened. You have no money and nowhere to go so you want to take a train ride out of town." I stared at him; he was good.

He smiled and boarded the train.

There was something about him. I had to know more. I bought my ticket and boarded, searching the train frantically for him. He was in the second carriage, reading a book. I guess it was a romance book: it was called Love at First Sight. I sat down next to him not knowing what I was going to say. He smiled and sat the book down. "You decided to take a train ride huh?" I nodded. I still had no words. I looked him over. He was well dressed and wore expensive shoes but no wedding ring.

He noticed I was looking him over, and he just grinned at me. I asked where he was going. "Heading home after work. I only got off at your stop to check if you were okay because I noticed you were crying." I managed to stutter out a thank you. He asked if I knew where I was going. I said "No, I'll probably get off where the train stops." He looked out the window at the darkness asking if I wanted to talk about what had happened.

What the hell, I needed to talk and I didn't know this guy from a bar of soap so why not pour my heart out to him. He pulled out a bottle of scotch from his briefcase, stating that it was a present and he doesn't drink and that I'm welcome to it if I wanted to drown my sorrows. I agreed and quickly skulled a quarter of the bottle and told him to put it back in his case before the ticket man came by to check the tickets. After a few minutes, the alcohol hit me and I started blurting out everything that had happened.

Two hours later, we arrived at the last stop where this man, I hadn't even got his name, was getting off. He helped me off the train. I was tipsy and groggy by this stage. I sat on the train station bench to get my bearings, and the next thing I knew I woke up on someone's couch.

Looking around the room, I could tell it was owned by the man from the train. He had pictures everywhere. But how had I gotten there? Hung-over and tired, I searched for his room to see if I could make a cup of coffee. The door of the room at the back of the house was slightly open; as I pushed it open. I got a shock: he was standing right in front of me stark naked. Man, he was a muscled punk. I hadn't noticed this with his clothes on. I came back to reality, embarrassed. He knew I was looking at him. He apologized, stating he sleeps naked. He moved in closer to me, and I noticed he looked pretty hard. Oh my god! He was coming onto me! I stepped back, asking why he hadn't tried this last night when I was nearly blind drunk.

He smiled and said, "I don't take

advantage of those situations. I think you're very attractive, but I wouldn't try to have sex with you when you're drunk."

He was sweet. He moved closer to me again and wrapped his arms around me and hugged me.

"Are you feeling better?"

"Still in a little bit of shock, but yes, I'm ok."

His hands moved from my waist so he was able to clutch my ass cheeks in his hands and pull me closer. I felt him hard against me, he starting kissing my neck and running his fingers down my stomach and then my thighs. I could feel him tugging at my underwear, but I pulled back. He grabbed me closer, feeling his hard erection against my clit.

"I cannot be unfaithful to my husband," I whispered.

"He fucked your sister, so I'm sure you can; let me show you like he never has."

With that, he slid his finger inside me. I gave an instant moan—that's my weak spot. I ran my hands across his erection as he lowered my pants and I soon saw them lying on the floor. He was moving his cock up and down along my clit while he inserted another finger nearly sending me to heaven. He had smooth soft hands but big fingers, and he knew how to use them.

I found myself moaning and groaning, horny as hell. He pushed me hard against the wall, and I opened my legs a little to allow him to enter. Taking out his fingers, he lifted me against the wall a little and slid his hard erection into my warm pussy. "Like a warm apple pie," I giggled.

He felt big; I hadn't had anyone this big before. He pushed me harder against the wall, penetrating me further, and he gently entered and then exited slowly.

He nibbled my lip; he knew how to tease. I felt hot and horny, but guilty because of my husband. I hadn't ever slept with anyone else. He scooped me gently in his arms and carried me to his bed. Lying on top of me, he leisurely took notice of my body, staring as he untied my bra one-handed. This guy was skilful.

I felt myself getting wetter; I wanted to keep fucking him. He lowered his tongue and slid down my chest, moving his body down as his tongue reached my clit. He looked up at me, asking if he could; I said no, but as he stuck two fingers inside of me anyway. I was screaming "Yes, yes do what you want." He was starting to pull my clit lips with his mouth, ever so gently. He got a little rougher as he slid his tongue inside my wet pussy. Fuck, it felt so good that I wanted his smooth warm tongue deeper. He ate me out until I was close to cumming, and then he reached around and pulled my ass towards him. Looking up at me, he asked me not to cum.

"I'm not done with you yet," he stated.

I was excited. He slid his cock up towards my face, pushing my big tits together. He inserted his dick and fucked my hook like he meant it; it felt good feeling him slip through each time. I felt more aroused. I could feel him pulsing as he fucked harder. He told me to open my mouth as he cummed. I caught it in my mouth, letting the salty nectar fill my mouth. His cream dripped down from my lips to my neck, revealing a pearl necklace all around my tits.

He smiled, telling me to brace for impact. He was going to bang my pussy hard and teach it a lesson. What? I couldn't believe this: he can go again straight after he's already blown. He's a sex god!

I didn't need lubrication; I was as wet as hell when he entered me as he pulled my legs apart. He pushed, penetrated, and lanced inside of me. He felt even bigger than before.

"Fuck me like a slut!" I yelled.

He penetrated harder; I could feel the pressure deep in me. Grabbing my arms, he pulled them behind my head and held them there. I couldn't do a thing. He fucked me stronger and faster. I couldn't move. He held a tight grip. I was patient; I let him finish. I let him do what he wanted to do.

He pulled out and flipped me over like a rag doll, telling me to jump on top and ride his horny dick. Sliding on top, I only sat on his dick, letting it insert a few centimetres, and then I rocked back and forth, letting him tell me how good this felt so I continued. I could feel my pussy creaming and his precum running onto his stomach. We were both wet as hell.

Sweat started lightly on my skin as I pushed his whole dick inside me, pushing as far as I could to get it right inside me. He moaned loudly as I motioned his hands to my tits for him to grope them gently, ordering him to grab my ass and spank it. He hit me hard, growling like an animal, throwing me off his dick. He edged my head towards his penis where I tasted sweet mixed juices with a savory taste. He held my head, guiding me in and out at his own pace before I stopped to let him ball sack my face.

After I ended up with cum all over my face, dripping wet, we both opted for a snack and a hot coffee down the local bakery. For only a short distance, we both walked, letting our bodies cool down. His arms looked even bigger, wearing nothing but nakedness. I eased back watching his ass walk in front of me. Oh my god! It turned me on.

He stopped and took my hand, and we walked hand in hand through the dry deserted track leading out to the bakery. After a cup of coffee and cake, we headed back through the track where he turned to me, held my chin in his hands, and asked if he could screw me down behind the evergreen tree. I was so hot I couldn't say no, hormones raging as we ripped each other's clothes off. He pushed me against the tree, sticking his cock in me so hard I groaned loudly.

He fucked me and fucked me, both of us cumming several times. Something about fucking outside turned me on. Perhaps it was the risk of getting caught?

He bent down and started to clean his cum inside me, and I felt it running everywhere.

Placing one leg over his shoulder, he inserted his tongue deeper, making his face a cream pie.

I wanted him to fuck my ass, which is something my husband never did. I sweetly asked him.

Without hesitation, he pulled my cheeks apart and slowly penetrated my ring hole. I felt a little tight until he got going at a quick motion. Fuck, it felt good! He pulled his cock out and slapped my ass cheeks with it before shoving it back inside me.

He fucked a lot quicker now as he was about to cum. He was so close; he sweetly asked if he was allowed to squirt in my ass. I gladly said yes.

Feeling him ejaculate in my ass was the best fucking feeling. I let it run out of me and we headed back for a shower.

On the way, he asked what I planned to do with my life now. I stayed silent.

I was offered a place in his bed if I wanted it; I thought this could be my fuck palace with my own personal sex god on demand.

He told me not to go back and to forget everything. He'd even bought a new handbag for me in case I wanted to do another train dash out of town.

I had a feeling this guy was a sweetheart: he was a great fuck buddy and was dirty and filthy but sweet as well.

Heading to the shower, I tied up my black locks into a loose ponytail, then stripped and stepped into the shower.

I had forgotten a towel. I called out asking if he could bring me a towel. He walked in naked, stating I could wear him as a towel. I got out of the shower a little cold as the air hit the water beads down my back, but I was soon bent over the bath getting fucked once again.

"Your pussy's going to get squirted."

I couldn't think of anything better. I craved his dick.

Standing up, he sucked my tits and tweaked my nipples, turning them all hard and erect. He started to finger me again, covering his fingers with mixed nectars, and then pushed the fingers inside my mouth, telling me to taste what he had done.

"Take it bitch. Suck those dirty fingers, you whore," he raged at me.

I didn't like this. I grabbed his erect cock and jerked it furiously until I started seeing his precum. I was obviously too good for him. I jerked it harder and harder and then sucked it. I then hammered his balls in my mouth; he was sweating a lot as he got closer to blowing. I moved my head up, opened my mouth, and waited to catch his delight in my mouth where I planned to keep it there while we French kissed.

It shot straight down my throat; still keeping a little, I ran my tongue up his stomach and then his chest and started kissing him roughly, spreading cum all over his face. He loved it.

My pussy was feeling numb, but I pursued his fingers down so I could feel them inside me again and again, sliding his fingers over my cunt's lips soft but sticky. This became boring; I wanted it hard core.

I went on all fours, sending my ass into his face.

"Lick my ass, then fuck it."

He became aroused as he started jerking off to my dirty words.

I clawed at the carpet as he fucked me from behind. My tits bounced up and down. I swayed myself and pushed back, helping his cock to penetrate me further.

I could feel his ball sack hitting my clit as we rocked back and forth furiously. My pussy was swelling, so I let my fingers arouse me, squeezing it, feeling my clit tighten around my fingers, sliding them in and out to the rhythm of our bodies rocking.

Perhaps my husband cheating with my sister gave me so much anger—so much fury I ended up fucking this guy's brains out. Usually I'd never think of having sex with someone I had just met, but that was because I never knew how hot it could be, especially sneaking around and screwing in every room in the house. He was hot; he owned the biggest cock in existence.

He was one of a kind who knew how to startle my nipples into mountains of erection. He panted as I sat in his lap and started playing with my clit; turning myself on, I mounted higher as I slowly bit his lip and nipped his ear. I whispered in his ear, "I love fucking myself with my fingers. Want to help me out?" His erection eloped again against my backbone as I helped him slide his rough thick fingers that sent my body through multiple orgasms. I couldn't reject the feeling. This man from the train turned me on and fucked me harder than I ever have been before.

I craved for more, shoving his fingers back into my tight pussy, begging him to let me cum all over his fingers. I moaned and fucked his fingers hard. As I squirted all over his fingers, he then rubbed my moisture down my breasts and over my nipples where he headed to kiss and caress them. My nipples were hard and sensitive to the friction of his tongue. I wanted him to fuck my ass again.

He pushed it in. I felt uncomfortable at first, but when he started thrusting rigorously, I felt like I was in heaven. "Harder, wilder," I screamed and he obeyed.

His cock ached as he released his load inside of me, letting it drip to the end of his knob as he pulled out of my tight ass. He rubbed his cum around my ring hole, then rubbed it onto my ass cheeks; cum is known for its moistening effects.

I licked my lips. What a fucking hot night! He cuddled me and kissed my cheek, asking if he had cheered me up. "Of course," I whispered. He went for a bath, telling me I was welcome to stay, but if not, I could take his business card resting on the top of his bedside table. He insisted that I call him anytime when I wanted a hot revenge fuck. I could tell this was going to be every weekend.

I decided to go back to my husband: never did he mention the flings with my sister; never did I mention my continual visits to the stranger I met on the train. In a way, I thought it enhanced our sex life as we both snuck around having sex with other people.

AUTHOR'S NOTE

Readers: I want to expand a few of the stories to see where the characters can be explored further. If there are any of the stories that you would like to read more about again, I'd love to hear from you!

Visit my blog at http://www.ariellefossett.com

Join my newsletter for free exclusive previews
http://www.ariellefossett.com/in

Follow me on Twitter at
http://www.twitter.com/ariellefossett

Like my page on Facebook at
http://www.facebook.com/ariellefossett

Discover my books at major ebook retailers everywhere.